U0025495

永恆的莎士比亞改寫劇本 ❻

暴風雨

THE TEMPEST

William Shakespeare ◆ 著

Brady Timoney ◆ 改寫 ｜ 李為堯 ◆ 譯

MP3

永恆的莎士比亞改寫劇本 ❻

暴風雨
THE TEMPEST

作　　者	William Shakespeare, Brady Timoney
翻　　譯	李為堯
編　　輯	王婷葦
校　　對	許書銘（第一幕至第二幕第一場）
	詹雅鈞（第二幕第二場至第五幕）
內文排版	劉秋筑
封面設計	林書玉
製程管理	洪巧玲
出 版 者	寂天文化事業股份有限公司
電　　話	+886-(0)2-2365-9739
傳　　真	+886-(0)2-2365-9835
網　　址	www.icosmos.com.tw
讀者服務	onlineservice@icosmos.com.tw
出版日期	2016 年 9 月 初版一刷

版權所有 請勿翻印
郵撥帳號 1998620-0 寂天文化事業股份有限公司
劃撥金額 600（含）元以上者，郵資免費。
訂購金額 600 元以下者，加收 65 元運費。
〔若有破損，請寄回更換，謝謝〕

國家圖書館出版品預行編目 (CIP) 資料

永恆的莎士比亞改寫劇本：暴風雨 / William Shakespeare,
Brady Timoney 作；李為堯譯.
-- 初版 .-- [臺北市]：寂天文化，2016.09
面；　公分
ISBN 978-986-318-496-6(平裝附光碟片)

873.43345　　　　　　　　　　　　　　105016401

Contents

Background. 4
Cast of Characters 5

ACT 1   Scene 1. 7
          Scene 2. 11

ACT 2   Scene 1. 45
          Scene 2. 62

ACT 3   Scene 1. 73
          Scene 2. 79
          Scene 3. 86

ACT 4   Scene 1. 93

ACT 5   Scene 1. 109

Epilogue ·125

中文翻譯 126
Literary Glossary 192

Background

Thanks to his scheming brother, Prospero has been banished as the Duke of Milan. For the past 12 years, he has lived on a deserted island with his daughter Miranda, now 15. Prospero's deep interest in study, the cause of his downfall in Milan, has ironically helped him to control the island through magic. Caliban, the deformed son of the dead witch Sycorax, is Prospero's unwilling servant. Ariel, a fairy who had been imprisoned in a pine tree by Sycorax, also serves Prospero. As the play opens, Prospero has caused a tempest at sea leading to the wrecking of a ship carrying his old enemies.

Cast of Characters

ALONSO: The King of Naples

SEBASTIAN: Alonso's brother

PROSPERO: The rightful Duke of Milan

ANTONIO: Prospero's brother, who has taken the position of the Duke of Milan

FERDINAND: The son of the King of Naples

GONZALO: An honest old counselor

ADRIAN and **FRANCISCO:** Lords

CALIBAN: A deformed slave

TRINCULO: A jester

STEPHANO: A drunken butler

CAPTAIN OF A SHIP

BOATSWAIN: The officer in charge of the deck's crew and equipment

SAILORS

MIRANDA: Prospero's daughter

ARIEL: An airy spirit

IRIS, CERES, JUNO, NYMPHS, REAPERS: Spirits

ACT 1

Summary

一艘船在暴風雨之中沉沒了，與此同時，在附近的小島上看著這一切發生的米蘭達，認為是她的父親運用法力造成這一場暴風雨，她因此哀悼生命的逝去。她的父親普洛斯帕羅則向她保證沒有任何人受傷，並揭曉了他們父女是如何被遺棄於這座島的故事。

十二年前，當米蘭達才不到三歲時，普洛斯帕羅貴為米蘭公爵，卻被他的弟弟安東尼奧與那不勒斯王阿隆佐設計，趕下了王位。他們只給普洛斯帕羅和米蘭達一艘沒有槳、沒有桅杆、沒有索具，也沒有滑車的破船，就將兩人放逐到海上自生自滅。若是沒有高貴的那不勒斯人貢札羅為他們準備了水、糧食、書籍與其他的補給品，他們不可能活得下來。這十二年以來，普洛斯帕羅憑藉著魔法，得到了魔法精靈愛麗兒，和出生在這個島上的畸形人類卡列班的幫助與臣服。

那不勒斯的王子菲迪南其實並沒有死在這場船難，就在米蘭達與普洛斯帕羅說話的同時，他來到了這兩人身邊。米蘭達與菲迪南一見鍾情，但普洛斯帕羅並不打算讓他們的愛情這麼唾手可得，他認為唯有經過磨難，愛情的果實才會更顯得甜美，於是他指控菲迪南其實是一名欲佔領這座島的間諜，並禁止米蘭達為其辯護。

Scene ❶ 🎧

A ship tosses and rocks during a storm. The **captain** and the **boatswain** come out on deck.

CAPTAIN: Boatswain!

BOATSWAIN: Here, Captain. How goes it?

CAPTAIN: Good fellow, speak to the sailors. Hurry, or we will soon run ourselves aground. Hurry!

(**Captain** exits, blowing his whistle. **Sailors** run by and start pulling at the sails.)

BOATSWAIN: Heave ho, my hearties! Work harder! Quickly! Take in the topsail. Obey the captain's whistle. *(Defiantly, to the storm):* Blow until you burst your lungs, as long as we can sail on.

(**Alonso** enters, along with **Sebastian, Antonio, Ferdinand, Gonzalo,** and **others**.)

ALONSO: Boatswain, where's the captain?

BOATSWAIN: Don't you hear him? You're in the way! Stay below. You're helping the storm.

GONZALO: No, good fellow, be patient.

7

BOATSWAIN: When the sea is! *(Pointing to the huge waves)* What do these care about kings? To your cabins! Silence! Get out of our way!

GONZALO: Good sir, remember who is on board.

BOATSWAIN: None that I love more than myself. You are a counselor. If you can command this storm to silence, do so. If not, give thanks that you have lived so long, and go to your cabin. Prepare for trouble, if it comes along.
(To the passengers): Get out of our way, I say!

(**Boatswain** exits, shouting orders.)

GONZALO: This fellow gives me great comfort. He wasn't born to be drowned— but hanged instead. Fate, stick to his hanging. Make the rope of his destiny our anchor, for our own is not helping us. If he has not been born to be hanged, we're in trouble.

(**Alonso** and **others** exit. **Boatswain** enters again.)

BOATSWAIN *(to sailors)*: Down with the topmast!
Quick! Lower, lower!

(Shouts are heard from the passengers below decks.)

Blast all this howling! They are louder
than the weather.

(**Sebastian**, **Antonio**, and **Gonzalo** enter again.)

You again? What are you doing here?
Shall we give up and drown? Do you
want to sink?

SEBASTIAN: May you choke, you bawling dog!

BOATSWAIN: Do some work, then.

ANTONIO: Hang, you dog! Hang, you
loudmouth! We are less afraid of
drowning than you are.

9

GONZALO: I guarantee he won't drown, even if the ship were no stronger than a nutshell.

BOATSWAIN *(to the sailors):* Heave ho! Raise the mainsail! Out to sea again. Turn her around!

(**Sailors** enter, soaking wet and frightened.)

SAILORS: All is lost. Say your prayers! It's hopeless. *(Sailors exit.)*

GONZALO: The king and the prince are at prayers. Let's join them. It seems to be our only hope.

(A confused noise is heard. "Mercy on us! Farewell, my wife and children. Farewell, brother! Oh, no! The ship is splitting up, splitting up!")

ANTONIO: Let's all go down with the king.

SEBASTIAN: We must say farewell to him.

(**Antonio** and **Sebastian** exit.)

GONZALO: Now I would give a hundred miles of sea for an acre of barren ground! God's will be done! But I would much rather die a dry death.

(**Gonzalo** exits.)

Scene ❷

An island. A cleared place before Prospero's cave.
Prospero and **Miranda** enter.

MIRANDA: My dearest father, if by your magic
  You have raised this storm, stop it now.
  The sky seems to be pouring down
    flaming tar,
  And the sea rises up to dash out the fire.
  Oh, I have suffered with those I saw suffer!
  A brave ship, which no doubt had some
  Noble people on board, was dashed to
    pieces.
  The cries broke my heart! Poor souls,
  they must surely have died!
  If I'd been a god with any power, I would
  Have sunk the sea into the earth. I would
    never
  Have let it swallow the good ship and
  The cargo of souls within her!

PROSPERO: Calm down. Don't be so upset.
  Tell your tender heart there's no harm done.

MIRANDA: Oh, this is a terrible day!

PROSPERO: No harm. I have done nothing
But what's best for you, my dearest
daughter.
You don't know who you are, nor where
I came from. You do not yet know that
I am greater
Than just Prospero, your humble father
Who lives in a humble cave.

MIRANDA: I never thought I should know more.

PROSPERO: It's time I tell you. Lend me a hand.
Help me remove my magic cloak.

(She does so, and he places it on a rock.)

Wipe your eyes. Take comfort.

The dreadful sight of the wreck harmed
no one.
Not even a hair has been hurt on any
creature
You heard crying or saw sinking into the sea.
Sit down. Now you must know more.

MIRANDA: You have often begun to tell me
What I am. But you always stopped and
Left my questions unanswered, saying,
"No more. Not yet."

PROSPERO: The hour has now come.
The very minute tells you to listen.
Now pay attention. Can you remember
A time before we came to this cave?
I do not think you can, for then you
were not
Quite three years old.

MIRANDA: Certainly, sir, I can.

PROSPERO: What can you remember?
Some other house or person?

MIRANDA: It's far off and rather like a dream.
Did I not have four or five women once
to look after me?

PROSPERO: You did, and more, Miranda.

But how is it that this lives in your mind?

What else can you see in that dim past?

If you remember things before you
came here,

How you came here might come back
to you.

MIRANDA: But I do not.

PROSPERO: Miranda, just twelve years ago,
your father

Was the Duke of Milan and a powerful
prince.

MIRANDA: Sir, are you not my father?

PROSPERO: Your mother was a masterpiece
of Virtue,

And she said you were my daughter.

Your father was the Duke of Milan.

His only heir was a princess, equally noble.

MIRANDA: My heavens! What foul play

Did we suffer, that we came to this place?

Or was it something good that we did?

PROSPERO: Both, both, my girl!
We were exiled by foul play, as you said.
But we were helped here by Divine
Providence.

MIRANDA: Oh, Father, my heart bleeds to
think of
The trouble I must have been to you,
Which I don't remember.
Tell me more.

PROSPERO: My brother was called Antonio.
Oh, that a brother could be so wicked!
Next to you, I loved him more than
anyone.
I trusted him to manage my kingdom.
At that time, Milan was the leading
city-state, and
I was the ruling duke. My understanding of
The liberal arts was unequaled. Since
education
Was my obsession, I continued to study.
I left the business of government to my
brother
And became a stranger to my own court.

I was all wrapped up in my secret studies.
　　Your false uncle—are you listening to me?

MIRANDA: Sir, most carefully!

PROSPERO: He learned how to grant favors, and
　　How to deny them. He learned who to
　　　promote,
　　And who to cut down to size. In this way,
　　He won the loyalty of my supporters.
　　Having then both personal power
　　And control over officials, he alone could
　　　call the tune
　　In my kingdom. He became the ivy that
　　　hid my
　　Princely tree from view.
　　He sucked the very life out of it. Are you
　　　listening to me?

MIRANDA: Oh, good sir, I am!

PROSPERO: Listen well. I neglected my worldly
　　Duties and instead concentrated on
　　　bettering my mind.
　　This is what waked an evil nature in my
　　　false brother.

My trust, which had no limits, encouraged
An equal and opposite deceit in him.
He was made rich by my income
And powerful by the trust I put in him.
We had switched places, and he took on
My royal duties, with all their privileges.
He began to think like a man who believes
His own lies—that *he* was indeed the duke.
In this way, his ambition grew. Do you hear?

MIRANDA: Your tale, sir, would cure deafness.

PROSPERO: He wanted to be the real duke!
As for me, poor fool, my library seemed
Dukedom enough. Soon he began to think
I was not able to handle my affairs.
    Eager for power,
He allied himself with the King of Naples.
He agreed to pay him taxes and to
Follow his leadership. He subjected Milan,
Up to then proudly independent, to the
Humiliation of being controlled by Naples.
Alas, poor Milan!

MIRANDA: Oh, in the name of heaven!

PROSPERO: Note the conditions of the treaty
And the results. Then tell me if this is the
work of a brother.

MIRANDA: I'd be wrong to think less than nobly
Of my grandmother.
Good mothers have given birth to bad sons.

PROSPERO: Now the treaty. This King of Naples,
Being an old enemy of mine,
Listened to my brother's idea. My brother
Would give him homage and money—
I don't know how much. In return, the king
Would instantly expel me and my family
From Milan and give my title to my
brother.
Then, a treacherous army was raised.
One fatal midnight, Antonio opened
The gates of Milan. In the dead of darkness,
His henchmen hurried us out—
Me and your crying self.

MIRANDA: Alas, for pity's sake!
Not remembering how I cried out then,
I will cry all over again. It is a tale
That brings tears to my eyes.

18

PROSPERO: Hear a little more.

Then I'll bring you to this latest business

Which is now upon us. Without it, this story

Would not even matter.

MIRANDA: Why did they not kill us, then?

PROSPERO: A good question, my girl.

Dear, they didn't dare. My people loved me

Too much, and they didn't want their foul

Deed to be marked with blood.

In short, they hurried us aboard a boat and

Took us several miles out to sea. There

A rotten carcass of a ship awaited us.

It had no rigging, tackle, sail, or mast.

Even the rats had left it. There they put us,

To cry to the sea that roared to us,

To sigh to the winds that sighed back to us.

MIRANDA: Alas, what trouble was I to you then!

PROSPERO: Oh, you were an angel who saved me.

All the while you smiled, divinely brave,

While I sprinkled the sea with salty tears

And groaned in misery.

MIRANDA: How did we reach the shore?

PROSPERO: By Divine Providence.

We had some food and fresh water given

To us by a noble Neapolitan, Gonzalo.

He also gave us fine clothes, linens, and

Other supplies that have since been useful.

And out of the kindness of his heart,
knowing how dearly

I loved my books, he brought me volumes
from

My own library that I prize above my
dukedom.

MIRANDA: I hope to see that man someday!

PROSPERO: Listen to the last of our sea-sorrow.
We got to this island. Here, as your teacher,
I've given you a fine education—much better
Than that of other princesses who have
More time for foolishness and
Whose tutors are not so careful.

MIRANDA: Heaven thank you for it! And now,
Please, sir—for it is still on my mind—what
Was your reason for raising this sea-storm?

PROSPERO: I will tell you this much.
By a strange accident, good Fortune,
which is
Now on my side, has brought my enemies
To this shore. And by my gift of second
sight,
I know that my lucky stars are shining
on me now.
I must seize upon this opportunity.
If I do not,
My fortunes will ever after droop.
No more questions for now.

(He passes his hands across her eyes.)

You feel sleepy. It is a good feeling.
Give in to it. I know you cannot choose.

(Miranda falls asleep.)

Come here, servant, come. I am ready now.
Approach, my Ariel. Come!

(**Ariel**, a spirit, enters.)

ARIEL: All hail, great master! Learned sir, hail!
I come to do your bidding, whether it be
to fly,
To swim, to dive into the fire, or to ride
On the curled clouds. Ariel and all of his
fellow spirits
Are at your service.

PROSPERO: Spirit, have you caused the tempest
That I ordered?

ARIEL: In every detail. I boarded the king's ship.
At the prow, below decks, on deck,
And in every cabin, I struck terror.
I appeared as separate flames, and then
I'd meet and join as one. Lightning flashes,
Which preceded the dreadful thunder claps,
Were never more frequent and bright.

The fire and cracks of thunder seemed to
Besiege even the mighty sea-king, Neptune,
And make his bold waves tremble.

PROSPERO: Brave spirit! Who could be so strong
That this uproar would not infect his reason?

ARIEL: Every soul aboard felt a touch of madness
And acted with desperation. All but the
sailors
Plunged into the foaming brine and left
the ship,
Which was burning at the time with my fire.
The king's son, Ferdinand, with his hair
Standing up—it was like reeds, not hair—
Was the first man to leap. He cried,
"Hell is empty. All the devils are here!"

PROSPERO: Why, that's my spirit!
But wasn't this near shore?

ARIEL: Close by, my master.

PROSPERO: And are they safe, Ariel?

ARIEL: Not a hair on their heads was harmed.
As you ordered, I've spread them about
the island in groups.

The king's son I have landed by himself.
I left him sighing away in an odd corner
Of the island, sitting with his arms folded
In a sad knot like this. *(He demonstrates.)*

PROSPERO: What have you done with the ship,
The sailors, and the rest of the fleet?

ARIEL: The king's ship is safely in harbor.
It is in the deep cove, where you once called
Me at midnight to fetch magic dew from the
Stormy Bermudas. The sailors are stowed
Under hatches below decks. I have cast a
Sleep spell on them, for they need the rest.
As for the rest of the fleet, which I scattered,
They have now met again and are on the
Mediterranean Sea. All are sadly bound
  home for Naples.
They are sure that they saw the king's
Ship wrecked and the king himself drowned.

PROSPERO: You've done exactly as I ordered.
But there's more work to do, Ariel.
  What time of day is it?

ARIEL: Past midday.

24

PROSPERO: At least 2:00. Between now and 6:00,
The time must be spent most wisely.

ARIEL: More work? Since you ask so much,
Let me remind you of what you promised—
Which hasn't yet been granted.

PROSPERO: What? Moody? What can you want?

ARIEL: My liberty.

PROSPERO: Before your time is up? Let's hear
no more of that!

ARIEL: With all due respect,
Remember that I have done as you asked.
I have told you no lies, made no mistakes,
Served without grudge or grumblings.
You did promise to release me a year early.

PROSPERO: Do you forget the torment
From which I freed you?

ARIEL: No.

PROSPERO: You have! Now you think it is
Too much to walk on the ocean's floor,
To run upon the sharp wind of the North,
To do my bidding in the deep waters
When the earth is hard with frost.

ARIEL: I do not, sir.

PROSPERO: You lie, you evil thing!
Have you forgotten the foul witch Sycorax,
Who was bent double with age and envy?
Do you not remember her?

ARIEL: I do, sir.

PROSPERO: You have *forgotten*! Where was she
born?
Speak. Tell me!

ARIEL: Sir, in Algiers.

PROSPERO: Oh, was she really? Once each month
I must go over what you have been,
Which you forget. You know that
This evil witch Sycorax was banished

From Algiers for countless misdeeds and
Terrible sorceries unfit for the human ear.
They wouldn't take her life
Because of one thing. Isn't this true?

ARIEL: Yes, sir.

PROSPERO: This blue-eyed hag was pregnant
  when
She was brought here by the sailors. You—
My "slave," as you describe yourself—
Were then her servant. Because you were
Such a sensitive spirit, you refused to
  carry out
Her gross and disgusting commands.
For this, she, in an uncontrollable rage,
  imprisoned you
In a split pine tree. With the help of
  her more
Powerful assistants, you remained there
Most painfully for twelve years. During
  that time,
She died and left you there. You groaned
As fast as mill wheels strike the water.
At that time, there were only two humans

On the island—you and the freckled son
To whom she had given birth.

ARIEL: Yes. Caliban, the witch's son.

PROSPERO: The *dunce*! That's who I mean:
That Caliban who is now my servant.
You know best the torment in which
I found you. Your groans did make the
Wolves howl. They touched the hearts
Of the ever-angry bears. It was a torment
Of the damned, which Sycorax
Could not reverse. It was *my* magic art,
When I arrived and heard you, that opened
The pine tree and let you out.

ARIEL: I thank you, master.

PROSPERO: If you complain again, I'll split
  an oak
And lock you in its knotty insides.
You can stay there until you have howled
  away twelve winters!

ARIEL: Your pardon, master!
I'll obey your commands
And do my duties graciously.

28

PROSPERO: Do so—and two days from now
I will set you free.

ARIEL: That's my noble master!
What shall I do? Tell me. What shall I do?

PROSPERO: Go make yourself into a sea nymph.
Be invisible to everyone but you and me.
Go, take this shape, and come back in it.
Leave now, and do as I say.

(**Ariel** exits. Prospero turns to the sleeping Miranda.)

PROSPERO: Awake, dear heart, awake.
You have slept well. Awake.

MIRANDA: Your story made me sleepy.

PROSPERO: Shake it off. Come on.
We'll visit Caliban, my slave, who never
Gives us a kind word.

(He turns to the opening of a nearby cave.)

MIRANDA: He's a villain. I don't like to see him!

PROSPERO: Yet even so, we cannot do without
his help.
He does make our fire, fetch our wood,
And perform services that help us.
(Calling out) Hey, there! Slave! Caliban!

You clod, you! Answer.

CALIBAN *(from inside the cave)*: There's enough
   wood inside.

PROSPERO: Come out, I say!

   Come, you tortoise! How much longer?

(**Ariel** enters, looking like a sea nymph.)

   A fine sight!

   My skillful Ariel, a word in your ear.

(He whispers in Ariel's ear.)

ARIEL: My lord, it shall be done.

(**Ariel** exits.)

PROSPERO *(to Caliban)*: You poisonous slave,
  Fathered by the devil himself upon your
  Wicked mother! Come out!

(**Caliban**, an ugly and deformed creature, enters.)

CALIBAN: May a wicked dew
  From rotten bogs drop on you both!
  May a hot wind blow and blister you all over!

PROSPERO: For saying that, be sure of this:
  Tonight you shall have cramps,
    side-stitches
  That will cut your breath short.
  Goblins shall pinch you all night long.
  Your skin will look like a honeycomb,
  Each pinch worse than a bee sting.

CALIBAN: I must eat my dinner.
  This island is mine, by Sycorax my mother,
    And you've taken it from me.
  When you first came here, you stroked me
  And made much of me. You'd give me water
  With berries in it. You taught me what
  To call the big light that burns during the day,

And what to call the smaller lights at night.
Then I loved you and showed you
All the features of the island—
The fresh springs and the salt pits,
The barren places and the fertile ones.
 Cursed may I be for doing so!
May all the spells of Sycorax—
Toads, beetles, and bats—fall on you!
I am all the subjects that you have—
I, who was once my own king! You pen me
In this hard-rock cave, while you keep
 from me
The rest of the island.

PROSPERO: You lying slave!
Whipping works with you, not kindness.
Filth though you are, I have treated you
With gentle care! I even let you sleep
In my own cave, until you tried
To violate my daughter's honor!

CALIBAN: Oh ho! Oh ho! I wish I had!
You stopped me. Otherwise, I would have
Populated this island with Calibans!

MIRANDA: You disgusting slave!

Goodness has no effect on you.

You are all evil. I pitied you and

Took the trouble to teach you to speak.

Not an hour passed that I didn't teach you

One thing or another. At that time, savage,

You didn't know your own thoughts, but

Would babble like a brute. I gave you

The words to make your thoughts known.

But your vile race, even though you did learn,

Had something in it that decent people

Could not bear. Therefore, you were

Rightly confined into this cave, though you

Deserved more punishment than this prison.

CALIBAN: You taught me language. My profit

From it is that I know how to curse.

May the plague with its red sores destroy you

For teaching me your language!

PROSPERO: Get away, you son of a witch!

Fetch us some wood, and be quick about it.

(Caliban shrugs to show his indifference.)

Do you shrug your shoulders, you evil thing?

If you disobey me, or work unwillingly,

I'll wrack you with cramps,

Fill all your bones with aches, make you roar

So loud that beasts will tremble at your noise.

CALIBAN *(shrinking in fear)*: No, please don't.

(aside): I must obey. His magic is so

powerful

It could even control Setebos,

my mother's god,

And make a servant of him.

PROSPERO: So, slave—go!

(**Caliban** exits. **Ferdinand** enters, followed by **Ariel**, who is invisible to all but Prospero. Ariel is playing a lute.)

ARIEL *(singing)*: *Come to these yellow sands*

And then take hands.

Curtsy next, and kiss. This will

Make the wild waves be still.

Step lightly here, and there,

And sweet spirits will sing the chorus.

Hark, hark . . .

CHORUS: *Bow-wow! The watchdogs bark!*

Bow-wow.

ARIEL: *Hark, hark, I hear the rooster crying.*

Cock-a-doodle-doo.

34

FERDINAND: Where is this music coming from,
   The air, or the earth?
   (He listens carefully.) It has stopped.
   Surely, it entertains some god of this island,
   Sitting on a bank, weeping yet again
   About the wreck of the king, my father.
   This music has calmed both me and the
      wild waters
   With its sweet melody. I have followed
      it here
   Or, rather, it has drawn me, but it is gone.
   No! It begins again.

ARIEL: *Five fathoms deep your father lies,*
His bones have coral made.
Those are pearls that were his eyes.
Everything about him has decayed
And suffered a complete change
Into something rich and strange.
Sea nymphs ring his death knell.

CHORUS: *Ding dong.*

ARIEL: Listen! *Now I hear them, ding-dong bell.*

FERDINAND: The song tells of my drowned father.
This is not a natural thing, nor any sound
The earth has heard. I hear it now above me.

PROSPERO *(to Miranda)*: Open your eyes,
And tell me what you see over there.

MIRANDA *(admiring Ferdinand)*: What is it?
A spirit? Lord, how it looks around.
Believe me, sir, it has a very handsome form.
But it is a spirit.

PROSPERO: No, my girl. It eats and sleeps and
Has the same senses that we have.
This gentleman you see was in the shipwreck.
Except for being somewhat stained with grief,

Which is bad for beauty, you might call him
A handsome person. He has lost his friends
And is wandering about to find them.

MIRANDA: I might call him a divine thing,
For I never saw anything on earth so noble!

PROSPERO *(aside):* It's turned out as I'd hoped!
(to Ariel): Spirit, fine spirit, I'll free you
Within two days for this!

FERDINAND *(seeing Miranda):* Surely this must be
The goddess for whom this music was
played.
(to Miranda): May I humbly ask to know
If you live upon this island? And please
    tell me
How I should conduct myself here. And lastly,
Oh, you marvel, here is my main question:
Are you a mortal young maiden or not?

MIRANDA: No marvel, sir, but certainly a
maiden.

FERDINAND: My own language? Heavens!
If I were now where it is spoken, I would be
The highest rank of them who speak it.

PROSPERO: What, the highest? What would
you be
If the King of Naples heard you?

FERDINAND: A lonely man, as I am now, who is
Surprised to hear you speak of Naples.
He does hear me, and because he does,
I weep—because I *am* the King of Naples.
With my own eyes, which have been weeping
Ever since, I saw the king, my father,
Go down in a shipwreck.

MIRANDA: Oh, how terrible!

FERDINAND: Yes indeed, and all his lords,
The Duke of Milan and his brave son
Being two of them.

PROSPERO *(aside)*: The real Duke of Milan
and his
Even braver daughter could prove you wrong
If now were the right time to do it.
(observing Ferdinand and Miranda) It is love
At first sight. Sweet Ariel, I'll free you for this.
(to Ferdinand): A word, good sir.
I think you are wrong. A word with you . . .

MIRANDA: Why does my father speak so rudely?
This is only the third man I have ever seen,
The first I ever sighed for. May pity move
My father to see things my way!

FERDINAND: Oh, if you are a virgin
And your love is not pledged to another,
I'll make you the Queen of Naples!

PROSPERO: Enough of that, sir. A word . . .
(aside) Each is infatuated with the other,
So I must make it more difficult for them.
Otherwise, an easy win will make the
Prize seem less valuable.
(to Ferdinand): Another word with you.
I insist that you
Listen to me: You are a fraud, and you have
Come here as a spy, to win this island
From me, the lord of it.

FERDINAND: No, upon my word of honor!

MIRANDA: No evil could live in such a temple!
If the evil spirit were so handsomely
housed,
Good things would want to dwell in it!

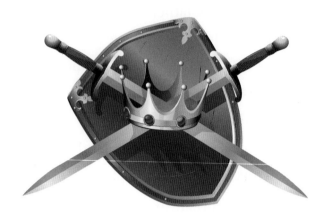

PROSPERO *(to Ferdinand):* Follow me.

> *(to Miranda):* Do not speak up for him.
>
> He's a traitor.
>
> *(to Ferdinand):* Come. I'll chain your neck
> and feet together.
>
> You shall drink sea water. Your food shall be
> Freshwater mussels, withered roots,
> And acorn husks. Follow me!

FERDINAND: No! I will resist such entertainment

> Until my enemy has more power.

(He draws his sword, but Prospero casts a spell on him
so he cannot move.)

ACT 1
SCENE 2

MIRANDA: Oh, dear father,

Don't treat him so harshly. He is a

gentleman

And he has not harmed you.

PROSPERO: What? Do you think my brains

Are in my feet?

(to Ferdinand): Put away your sword, traitor.

You make a show,

But you dare not strike. Your conscience is

Full of guilt. I can disarm you with this stick

(He flicks his magic wand, knocking away Ferdinand's
sword.)

And make your weapon drop.

MIRANDA: I beg you, Father.

PROSPERO: Get away! Don't pull my clothes!

MIRANDA: Sir, have pity! I'll vouch for him.

PROSPERO: Silence! One word more

Shall make me scold you, if not hate you.

What? Defend an impostor? Quiet!

You think there are no more like him?

Foolish girl!

Compared to most men, he is like a Caliban,

And most men are like angels compared to
   him.

MIRANDA: My tastes are then most humble.
   I have no ambition to see a handsomer man.

PROSPERO *(to Ferdinand):* Come now, obey me.
   Your muscles are like those of a baby.
   They have no strength in them.

FERDINAND: So they are. My senses are all numb,
   As in a dream. The loss of my father,
   The weakness that I feel, the shipwrecking
   Of all my friends, and this man's threats—
   They all mean nothing to me if only I
      might look upon
   This maiden from my prison once a day.
   Let free men make use of all the other corners
   Of the Earth. I would have space enough
   In such a prison.

PROSPERO *(aside):* It's working.
   (to Ferdinand): Come on.
   (to Ariel): You've done well,
   Fine Ariel. Follow me. Listen to what else
   You can do for me.

MIRANDA *(to Ferdinand):* Be comforted.
My father really has a better nature than
You might think. This is unusual behavior.

PROSPERO *(to Ariel):* You shall be as free
As mountain winds. But do exactly as I say.

ARIEL: To the last syllable.

PROSPERO *(to Ferdinand):* Come, follow me.
(to Miranda): Do not speak on his behalf.

(**All** exit.)

ACT 2

Summary

其他的船難生還者聚集在島的另一隅，
貢札羅讚嘆著島嶼的美麗，阿隆佐則
為他以為已淹死的兒子菲迪南哀悼。不久之後，除了瑟拜士梯安與安東尼奧之外的人都陷入了沉睡，安東尼奧慫恿瑟拜士梯安殺了阿隆佐與其他人，這樣他就可以不用再臣服於那不勒斯，並自稱為米蘭王。

就在他們打算付諸行動時，愛麗兒在貢札羅耳邊歌唱喚醒了他與其他人，阿隆佐質問安東尼奧為何拔出了他的劍，瑟拜士梯安強辯說是因為聽到附近有野獸的聲音。

在島的另外一邊，卡列班正扛著木材，就看到小丑屈林鳩羅朝他走來，他以為屈林鳩羅是普洛斯帕羅派來折磨他的，因此他躺平在地上，並將自己隱藏在斗篷之下。屈林鳩羅聽著雷聲就在不遠處，決定趕緊找個地方躲避這場風暴，所以他也躲進了卡列班的斗篷之下。

斯蒂芬諾帶著一瓶酒來到這裡，看到了他以為是兩個頭、四隻腳的怪物，他決心要馴養這頭怪物並帶他回那不勒斯。於是他餵給了卡列班一些酒，就在他也要餵酒給屈林鳩羅時，屈林鳩羅說話了。很快斯蒂芬諾就明白這並不是一隻四腳的怪物，屈林鳩羅只不過是另一個船難的生還者。他們都喝了酒，卡列班願意服侍斯蒂芬諾以換得更多的美酒。

Scene ❶ 🎧 ⑸

Another part of the island. **Alonso, Sebastian, Antonio, Gonzalo, Adrian, Francisco**, and other **survivors** enter.

GONZALO: I beg you, men, be merry.
We all have cause for joy. Our escape
is worth much more than our losses.
Every day, some sailor's wife, ship owners, and
Merchants have the same reason for sorrow
That we have. But few people in millions
Can claim the good luck we've had in
surviving.
So, dear friends, we must weigh our
sorrow against our luck.

ALONSO: Please, be quiet!

SEBASTIAN *(aside to Antonio):* He receives comfort
like cold porridge.

ANTONIO *(to Sebastian, sneering at Gonzalo):*
The social worker will not give up so easily.

SEBASTIAN *(to Antonio, agreeing):* Look,
He's winding up the watch of his wit.
(Gonzalo thinks hard about what to say.)
Any minute now, it will strike.

GONZALO *(to Alonso)*: Sir, when one has
Experienced every possible grief,
There comes to the entertainer—

SEBASTIAN: His fee. A dollar piece?

GONZALO: Peace does come to him, indeed.
You have spoken more truly than you knew.

SEBASTIAN: You've taken it more wisely than I
expected.

GONZALO: So, my lord—

ANTONIO: My, he does go on and on!

ALONSO *(to Gonzalo)*: Please, sir, calm down.

GONZALO: I'll say no more, but yet—

SEBASTIAN: He will go on talking!

ANTONIO *(to Sebastian)*: For a good bet, which
of the two—Gonzalo or Adrian—will
start crowing first?

SEBASTIAN *(whispering back)*: Gonzalo!

ANTONIO: Adrian!

SEBASTIAN: Done! *(They shake on it.)* The bet?

ANTONIO: Just for the fun of it.

SEBASTIAN: It's a deal!

ADRIAN: Though this island seems deserted—

ANTONIO *(laughing):* Ha, ha, ha!

SEBASTIAN *(to Antonio):* So, you win the bet!

ADRIAN *(continuing):* And difficult to reach—

SEBASTIAN *(whispering to Antonio):* Yet—

ADRIAN: Yet—

ANTONIO *(whispering back to Sebastian):* He was bound to say that!

ADRIAN *(unaware that Sebastian and Antonio are mocking him):* The weather seems to be mild, sweet, and delicate.

ANTONIO *(nudging Sebastian):* I once knew a girl like that!

SEBASTIAN: A real charmer, as he so wisely said.

ADRIAN: The air here breathes so sweetly.

SEBASTIAN *(to Antonio):* As if it had rotten lungs.

ANTONIO *(replying):* Or came from a swamp.

GONZALO: Everything one might wish is here.

ANTONIO *(aside):* True, all but the means to live.

SEBASTIAN *(aside):* There's none, or little, of that!

GONZALO: How lush and healthy the grass looks!

ANTONIO *(aside)*: Actually, the land is parched.

SEBASTIAN *(aside)*: With just patches of green.

ANTONIO *(aside)*: He doesn't miss much.

SEBASTIAN *(aside)*: No, just the whole truth . . .

GONZALO: But the amazing thing is—and it's almost beyond belief—

SEBASTIAN *(aside)*: As most amazing things are.

GONZALO: —that our clothes, though they were drenched in the sea, are still fresh.

ANTONIO *(aside)*: What fantastic statement will he make next?

SEBASTIAN *(aside)*: He'd put this island in his pocket and give it to his son as an apple.

ANTONIO *(aside)*: And by sowing the seeds of it in the sea, he will bring forth more islands.

GONZALO *(to Alonso)*: Isn't my jacket as fresh as the day I first wore it at your daughter's wedding in Tunis?

ALONSO: I wish I'd never come on this voyage to see my

Daughter married to the King of Tunis.

Coming home, my son has been lost!

And, in my opinion, she is lost, too.
Now she lives so far away from Italy
That I fear I shall never see her again!
Oh, my son and heir of Naples and of Milan,
What strange fish has made a meal of you?

FRANCISCO: Sir, he may still be alive.
I saw him strike out strongly
And ride the waves that were under him.
He stayed afloat, keeping his bold head
Above the challenging waves. I do not doubt
That he reached land alive.

ALONSO: No, no, he's gone, gone!

SEBASTIAN: Sir, you may thank yourself for
This great loss. You would not bless
Our Europe with your daughter. Instead,
You chose to let her marry an African.
You may never see her again, which is
Enough cause for your weeping!

ALONSO: Please, be quiet.

SEBASTIAN: We all begged you to do otherwise.
The poor girl was torn between wanting
To marry and wanting to obey you,

Not knowing which to choose. Now, I fear,
We have lost your son forever.
Because of this business, Milan and Naples
Now have more widows than there are men
To comfort them. The fault is your own!

ALONSO: So is the greatest loss.

GONZALO: Lord Sebastian, the truth you speak
Is lacking in gentleness and poorly timed.
You rub the sore when you should be
Bringing the medicine.

SEBASTIAN: You are right.

ANTONIO: Just like a surgeon!

GONZALO: Your cloudy mood brings
Foul weather to all of us, good sir.

SEBASTIAN: Foul weather?

ANTONIO: Very foul.

GONZALO *(ignoring them)*: If I settled on this
island, my lord—

ANTONIO *(aside)*: He'd sow it with nettles.

SEBASTIAN *(aside)*: Or weeds or herbs.

GONZALO: In my perfect country, I'd do all

In opposites. There would be no judges.

Learning would be unknown. Riches,
 poverty,

And slavery—there would be none.

No contracts, no inheritance, no boundaries,

No fences, no farming, and no vineyards.

There'd be no use of metal, corn, wine, or oil.

And no one would have an occupation.

All men would be idle. And all women, too,

But innocent and pure. No king—

SEBASTIAN *(aside):* Yet he said *he'd* be the king!

ANTONIO *(aside):* The final details of his
 country don't agree with the first ones.

THE
TEMPEST

GONZALO: Nature would provide for us without
Sweat or work, for the common good.
There would be no treason, crime, swords,
Spears, knives, guns, or artillery.
Nature would bring forth all crops
And harvests to feed my innocent people.
I would govern so perfectly, sir,
That it would be better than the Golden Age.

SEBASTIAN: God save his majesty!

ANTONIO: Long live Gonzalo! *(They laugh at him.)*

GONZALO: And—are you listening to me, sir?

ALONSO: I beg you, sir. Please, no more.
You are talking nonsense!

GONZALO: You are right, your highness. I did it
to amuse these gentlemen, who have such
sensitive and active lungs that they
always laugh at nothing.

ANTONIO: It was you we were laughing at.

GONZALO: In this kind of foolishness, I am
nothing compared to you. So continue.
Keep on laughing at nothing.

ANTONIO: What a witty blow!

SEBASTIAN *(continuing to mock Gonzalo):* And not with the flat side of the sword!

GONZALO: You are such strong gentlemen! You would lift the moon out of her orbit if she went five weeks without changing.

(**Ariel** enters, invisible, playing solemn music.)

ANTONIO *(to Gonzalo):* My lord, don't be angry.

GONZALO: Of course not. I wouldn't let such a little thing bother me. How about laughing me to sleep? I am very tired.

ANTONIO: Go to sleep. Listen to us. *(He laughs.)*

(Everyone falls asleep except Alonso, Sebastian, and Antonio.)

ALONSO: What, all asleep so soon? I wish I could Shut out my thoughts by shutting my eyes. They're inclined to close.

SEBASTIAN: Well then, sir, don't resist the feeling. Sleep seldom visits those in sorrow. When it does, it is a comfort.

ANTONIO: The two of us will guard you While you take your rest. We'll protect you.

ALONSO: Thank you. *(He yawns and stretches.)* I am amazingly sleepy. . . .

(He nods off quickly. **Ariel** exits.)

SEBASTIAN: What a strange drowsiness has
come over them!

ANTONIO: It's the air here.

SEBASTIAN: So why does it not make *us* sleepy?
I don't feel tired at all.

ANTONIO: I don't, either. I'm wide awake.
They all dropped off together, as if
They had all agreed to do so at the same time,
Or as if they were all hit by a thunderbolt.
(He pauses, thinking.) What if, Sebastian, oh,
What if—?

(He stops short, not daring to say what he thinks.)

I'd better say no more.
And yet, I think I can see in your face,
What you should be. In my imagination,
I can see a crown dropping on your head.

SEBASTIAN: What? Are you awake?

ANTONIO: Do you not hear me speak?

SEBASTIAN: I do, but surely you make no sense.
Are you talking in your sleep?
What did you say? This is a strange rest,

To be asleep with your eyes wide open—
Speaking, moving, and yet so fast asleep.

ANTONIO: Noble Sebastian, you are letting
Your fortune sleep—or should I say die!
Your eyes are shut while you are awake.

SEBASTIAN: Your snoring is clear.
There is meaning in your snores.

ANTONIO: I am more serious than I usually am.
You must be so, too, if you're thinking of
Taking my advice. But if you do, you'll be
Three times greater than you are now.

SEBASTIAN: Well, I am like still water—
Not inclined to go one way or the other.

ANTONIO: I'll teach you how to flow.

SEBASTIAN: Please go on. The look in your eye
And on your face hints that you have
Something important to say.
You seem almost ready to burst with it!

ANTONIO: It's this, sir. *(He nods at Gonzalo.)*
This forgetful old lord—who shall be
   forgotten
Himself when he is dead and buried—

Has almost persuaded the king
That his son is alive. It is as impossible
To believe that he didn't drown,
As it is to believe that he who is sleeping
  here is actually swimming.

SEBASTIAN: I have no hope that he has survived.

ANTONIO: Oh, out of that lack of hope for him,
What great hope comes for you?
No hope in one direction is, from another
Point of view, so high a hope that even
Ambition can't look that far ahead. Will you
Agree with me that Ferdinand is drowned?

SEBASTIAN: He's gone.

ANTONIO: Who's the next heir of Naples?

SEBASTIAN: Claribel.

ANTONIO: She who is now Queen of Tunis—
And now living 30 miles from nowhere.
She can't get news from Naples, unless the
Sun acts as the postman. The man in the moon
Is too slow. That same Claribel is the one
We were leaving when we were shipwrecked.
Some of us were cast here, destined to perform
An act in a drama. In that drama,

What's past is prologue. What's to come
Is to be acted out by you and me.

SEBASTIAN: What nonsense is this?
What are you saying? It is true that
My brother's daughter is the Queen of Tunis.
But she is also the heir of Naples.
The distance between is great.

ANTONIO: And every inch of that distance
Seems to cry out: "How can that Claribel
Ever get back to Naples? Stay in Tunis,
And let Sebastian wake up!" Suppose
These sleepers were dead—they'd be no worse
Than they are now. There is someone who can
Rule Naples as well as he who is sleeping.
There are plenty of lords who can prattle on
As much and as needlessly as this Gonzalo.
I could teach a parrot to speak at his level.
Oh, if only you thought the same way I do!
What a sleep this would be

(He points to Gonzalo, Alonso, Adrian, and Francisco.)

In terms of your future!
Do you understand me?

SEBASTIAN: I think I do.

ANTONIO: And what do you think of it?

SEBASTIAN: I remember how you overthrew
   your brother Prospero. . . .

ANTONIO: True. And look at how well
   my clothes fit me now—much better
   than before.
   My brother's servants were then my equals.
   Now they work for me.

SEBASTIAN: But what about your conscience?

ANTONIO: A good question, sir. Where is it?
   Twenty consciences could stand between
   Me and Milan. They could be frozen solid and
   Then melt before they would bother me.
   Here lies your brother, no better than
   The earth he lies upon.

(He draws a dagger.) With this obedient steel,
   I could lay him to bed forever.
While I do that, you could put this old man
(pointing to Gonzalo) To the endless 40 winks.
We don't want him to criticize our actions.
For all the rest, they'll lap up our story
As a cat laps up milk.
They'll go along with anything we say.

SEBASTIAN: Your example, dear friend,
   Will be my inspiration. As you got Milan,
   I'll come by Naples. Draw your sword.
   One stroke shall free you from the tributes
   That you pay—and I, the new king,
   Will be your dear friend.

ANTONIO: We'll draw our swords together.
   When I raise my hand, you do the same,
   And let it fall on Gonzalo.

SEBASTIAN: Just one word more . . .

(He takes Antonio to one side, where they talk. **Ariel**
enters, still invisible. He goes to Gonzalo.)

ARIEL: Through his magic art, my master
   foresees
   The danger that surrounds you.

He sends me forth to keep everyone alive.
Otherwise, his plan will fail.

(Ariel sings in Gonzalo's ear.)

While you here do snoring lie,
Conspiracy with an open eye
His chance does take.
If of life you have some care,
Shake off slumber, and beware.
Awake, awake!

ANTONIO *(returning, with his sword raised)*:
Then let us both be sudden!

GONZALO *(suddenly waking up)*: May the
Good angels preserve the king!

(The others awake and look around in surprise.)

ALONSO *(confused)*: What's going on?
(to Antonio): Why have you drawn your sword?
Why do you have such a ghastly look?

GONZALO: What's the matter?

SEBASTIAN *(dropping his sword and thinking quickly)*:
While we stood here guarding you,
We heard a hollow burst of bellowing.

It sounded like bulls, or maybe lions.

Didn't it wake you?

It struck my ears most terribly.

ALONSO: I heard nothing.

Did you hear this, Gonzalo?

GONZALO: Upon my honor, sir, I heard a
humming

(A strange one, too), which did awake me.

As I opened my eyes, I saw their weapons.

There was a noise, that's true. It's best that

We be on our guard or leave this place.

Let's draw our weapons.

ALONSO: Lead the way, and let's continue
Searching for my poor son.

GONZALO: May heaven keep him safe from
These beasts—for he's surely on this island.

ALONSO: Lead the way.

ARIEL: Prospero shall know what I have done.
King, go safely on to seek your son.

(**All** exit.)

Scene 2

Another part of the island. **Caliban** enters, carrying a load of wood. Thunder is heard in the distance.

CALIBAN: May all the infections the sun
  Has sucked from bogs and swamps
  Fall on Prospero—and give him a disease!

(**Trinculo**, a jester, enters.)

  Here comes one of his spirits, to torment me
  For bringing wood in slowly. I'll lie flat, and
  Hide under my cloak. Maybe he won't see me.

TRINCULO: There are no bushes or shrubs here
    to protect me from the weather, and
    another storm is brewing. I hear it in the
    wind. That huge black cloud looks like a
    rotten cask about to burst and shed its
    liquor. If it thunders, as it did before, I
    don't know where to hide my head. That
    same cloud is bound to rain pailfuls.

(He sees Caliban.)

  What have we here? A man or a fish?
    Dead or alive? A fish—he smells like a fish.
    He has a very ancient and fish-like smell.

62

A strange fish! If I were in England and had this fish painted on a sign, every fool would give me a piece of silver to see it. But they would not give a penny to relieve a lame beggar!

ACT 2
SCENE 2

(He looks more closely at Caliban.)

But wait! This is no fish! It looks like an islander, struck dead by a thunderbolt.

(Thunder is heard, louder now.)

Oh, no! The storm has returned. Where can I find shelter? Misery gives a man strange bedfellows. I will shelter with the dead man till the storm is past.

(He crawls under Caliban's cloak, until they are lying head to toe.)

(**Stephano** enters, singing, holding a bottle.)

STEPHANO *(singing):*
I shall no more go to sea, to sea.
Here shall I die, on the shore.
This is a lousy song to sing at a man's funeral.
(taking a drink) Well, here's my comfort.
(singing again) The captain, the crew, and I

Loved Molly, Meg, Marian, and Margerie,
But none of us cared for Kate.
For she had a tongue with a tang,
And would cry to a sailor, "Go hang!"
She hated the smell of tar and of pitch—
Though a tailor might scratch her wherever
*   she itched!*
So to sea, boys, and let her go hang!
This is a lousy song, too.

(He raises the bottle to his lips again.)

But here's my comfort!

CALIBAN *(to Trinculo)*: Don't torment me!
(He groans.) Oh!

STEPHANO: What's this? Do we have devils
here?

(He inspects the bundle on the ground, from which
two sets of legs—Caliban's and Trinculo's—stick out.)

Do you trick us, with savages and freaks? I
have not escaped drowning to be afraid
now of your four legs.

CALIBAN *(as Trinculo moves about)*: The spirit
torments me. Oh!

STEPHANO: This is some island monster who has a fever. Where did he learn our language? I will give him some medicine. If that's all that's wrong with him, maybe I can make him better, keep him tame, and take him to Naples. He'd be a good present for any emperor who ever wore shoes.

CALIBAN (*to Trinculo, pleading*): Do not torment me, I beg you. I'll bring the wood home faster.

STEPHANO: He's in a fit now and makes no sense. Let him have a taste from my bottle. If he has never had wine before, it will help end his fit. If I can cure him and tame him, I won't charge *too* much for him—just every penny I can get! (*approaching Caliban*) Come here. Open your mouth. Here is something to stop your shaking.

TRINCULO: I know that voice! It must be—but he is drowned. These are devils! Oh, help me!

STEPHANO: Four legs and two voices—what a monster! His front voice speaks well of

his friend, and his back voice utters foul
speeches. If it takes all the wine in my
bottle to do it, I will cure his fever.
Come. *(He pours wine down Caliban's throat.)*
That's enough. *(He moves to Trinculo.)* Now
I'll pour some into your other mouth.

TRINCULO: Stephano!

STEPHANO: Does your other mouth call me?
Mercy! This is a devil, and no monster!

TRINCULO: Stephano, if you are Stephano,
touch me and speak to me. I am
Trinculo. Don't be afraid. I am your good
friend, Trinculo.

STEPHANO: If you are Trinculo, come forth.
(He grips Trinculo's legs.)

I'll pull you by the two small legs. If any
belong to Trinculo, these do.
(Trinculo scrambles to his feet.)

Indeed, you are Trinculo! What are you
doing with this creature?

TRINCULO: I thought he'd been killed by a
thunderbolt. But weren't you drowned,

Stephano? Is the storm over? I hid under this dead monster's cloak, in fear of the storm. So you are alive, Stephano?

(He turns Stephano around to get a good look at him.)

STEPHANO: Please do not turn me about! My stomach is not settled!

CALIBAN *(aside)*: These are fine things, if they are not spirits. That's a brave god, and he carries heavenly liquor. I will kneel to him.

STEPHANO: How did you escape? Swear by this
bottle how you got here! I escaped on a
cask of wine, which the sailors threw
overboard. I made this bottle from the
bark of a tree, with my own hands, after
I was cast ashore.

CALIBAN *(at Stephano's feet)*: I'll swear on that
bottle, to be your true subject! That
liquor is heavenly!

STEPHANO *(handing the bottle to Trinculo as if it were
a Bible)*: Tell me, then, how you escaped.

TRINCULO: I swam ashore, man, like a duck.

STEPHANO *(offering Trinculo the bottle)*: Here, kiss
the Book. *(Trinculo drinks.)*

TRINCULO: Do you have any more of this?

STEPHANO: My wine is hidden in a cave by the
shore. *(noticing Caliban, at his feet)* Well,
now, monster! How's your fever?

CALIBAN: Have you dropped down from heaven?

STEPHANO: From the moon, I assure you.
I was the man in the moon, once.

CALIBAN: I have seen you in her, and I adore you.

STEPHANO *(offering more drink to Caliban)*: Come
on, swear to that. Kiss the Book.

(Caliban drinks some wine.)

I'll fill it soon with more wine.

TRINCULO: By this good light, I can see that
this is a very foolish monster. Me, afraid
of him? A very weak monster! *(He scoffs.)*
The man in the moon? A most foolish
monster!
(Caliban finally lowers the bottle.) Well drunk,
monster, for sure!

CALIBAN: I'll show you every fertile inch of the
island, and I will kiss your feet. Please,
be my god!

(He reaches out for the bottle as Stephano nods off.)

TRINCULO: He is a very wicked monster. When
his god's asleep, he robs his bottle.

CALIBAN: Let me kiss your feet. I'll swear
myself to be your subject.

STEPHANO: Come on, then. Down and swear!
(Caliban drops to his knees.)

TRINCULO: I'll laugh myself to death at this
empty-headed monster.

STEPHANO: Come on—kiss my hand!

TRINCULO: But the poor monster is drunk!
A disgusting monster!

CALIBAN: I'll show you the best springs.
I'll pick berries for you. I'll fish for you,
And find enough wood to warm you.
A plague on the tyrant that I serve.
I'll carry him no more wood,
But follow you instead, you wonderful man!

TRINCULO: A most ridiculous monster, to
worship a drunkard!

CALIBAN: Please, let me take you where
The apples grow. With my long nails,

I will dig you groundnuts.
I'll show you a jay's nest, and teach you
To trap a nimble little monkey. I'll bring you
Clusters of nuts, and sometimes
I'll get you young seagulls from the rocks.
Come with me.

STEPHANO: Please, lead the way without any
more talking. Trinculo, with the king and
the rest of our company drowned, you
and I will take over this island.

CALIBAN *(singing drunkenly)*: Farewell, master!

TRINCULO *(holding his hands over his ears)*: A
howling monster! A drunken monster!

CALIBAN *(singing)*: *I'll catch no more fish,*
Fetch no more wood, at his wish.
I won't scrape his bowls or wash a dish.
'Ban, 'Ban, Caliban,
Has a new master! Get a new man!
Freedom, happy day, happy day!
Freedom, freedom, happy day!

STEPHANO: Oh, brave monster! Lead the way!

(**All** exit.)

ACT 3

Summary

菲迪南正因為他的懲罰而扛著木材之時,米蘭達來找他,隱身的普洛斯帕羅也在一旁聽著兩人的談話,聽他們表白愛意與互定終生,普洛斯帕羅為此非常高興。

在島的另外一邊,卡列班、斯蒂芬諾與屈林鳩羅也在說話,卡列班勸斯蒂芬諾殺掉普洛斯帕羅,斯蒂芬諾為娶米蘭達並佔領整座島而同意了。

另外一邊,安東尼奧與瑟拜士梯安仍謀劃著要刺殺阿隆佐。與此同時,島上的精靈為這些人準備了一場盛宴,不過就在眾人準備大快朵頤之時,愛麗兒拍動著翅膀現身了。他撤掉了這些食物,並且宣讀了這些人的對普洛斯帕羅犯下的罪,這些人將為此永遠受苦受難。

愛麗兒消失之後,阿隆佐非常自責,他認為菲迪南會死都是他的錯,甚至想要與菲迪南一起死去。瑟拜士梯安與安東尼奧跟著他,似乎是想要確定他的死亡,貢札羅則命令其他人也跟上前去,避免這項悲劇的發生。

Scene ❶ 🎧

In front of Prospero's cave. **Ferdinand** enters, carrying a log.

FERDINAND: Some sports are painful, but the pain
Is rewarded by delight. Some humiliations
Are undergone with dignity. Most humble work
  has a worthy end. This, my lowly labor,
Would be heavy and unpleasant, except
For the mistress whom I serve. She brings
  life
To what's dead and makes my work a
  pleasure.
Oh, she is ten times gentler than her
  father is—
He is made up of harshness! I must move
Thousands of these logs, and pile them up,
Or risk punishment. My sweet mistress
Weeps when she sees me work. She says that
Such terrible work never had such a worker.
I'm daydreaming. But these sweet thoughts
Do make my work lighter.
I work harder when I daydream this way.

(**Miranda** enters, followed by Prospero, whom she
cannot see.)

MIRANDA: Alas, I beg you not to work so hard!
  I wish the fire of lightning had burned up
    those logs
  That you are forced to pile up! Please,
  Set that one down and rest a moment.
  My father is studying. Please, rest yourself!
  He'll be busy for the next three hours.

FERDINAND: Oh, dear mistress, the sun will set
  Before I finish what I must do.

MIRANDA: If you'll sit down, I'll carry the logs
  For a while. Please, give me that one.
  I'll carry it to the pile.

FERDINAND: No, precious one. I'd rather strain
  My muscles and break my back than have you
  Do such work while I sit idly by.

MIRANDA: It would suit me as well as it does you.
  And I would do it much more easily,
  For my heart is in it, but yours is not.

PROSPERO (overhearing): Poor creature,
  You have caught it badly. This proves it.

MIRANDA: You look tired.

FERDINAND: No, noble mistress. It's like
Fresh morning when you are near me
   at night.
I beg you—so I might use it in my prayers—
What is your name?

MIRANDA: Miranda.

FERDINAND: Admired Miranda!
Indeed the top of admiration!
Worth what's dearest to the world!
I have admired many a lady, and many times
Their sweet words have made me fall in love.
But never has one of them been so perfect
She didn't have some defect
That argued against her noblest graces.
But you—you are so perfect, so without
   equal!
You are created from the best of every
   creature!

MIRANDA: I do not know another woman.
I remember no woman's face but my own,
Which I see in my mirror. Nor have I seen

Any other men than you, good friend, and
My dear father. How other faces look,
I know not. But I would not wish for
Any companion in the world but you.

FERDINAND: In rank, Miranda, I am a prince,
And probably a king! I would no sooner
Carry this wood like a slave than I would
Allow a fly to enter my mouth.
Hear my soul speak: The instant I saw you,
My heart flew to your service. There it stays,
Making me a slave to it. For your sake,
I am this patient log-man.

MIRANDA: Do you love me?

FERDINAND: Heaven and earth be witness
To my words. If I speak the truth,
May my words be crowned with success.
If my words are hollow, may any good
That is in store for me turn to misfortune!
I love, prize, and honor you beyond the limit
Of everything that is in the world.

MIRANDA *(crying out):* I am a fool to weep at such
glad news!

PROSPERO *(aside)*: A joyous meeting of
Two loving souls! May the heavens bless
both of them!

FERDINAND: Why do you weep?

MIRANDA: At my unworthiness. I dare not
offer
What I want to give. Far less, can I take
What I cannot live without. But this is silly.
The more I try to hide things,
The more obvious they seem!
No more bashful riddles!
I will be your wife, if you will marry me.
If not, I'll die unmarried.

FERDINAND: My wife, dearest! And I am
humbly yours forever.

MIRANDA: My husband, then?

FERDINAND: Yes, with a heart as willing as a slave
Who wants freedom. Here is my hand.

MIRANDA: And here is mine, with my heart in it.
And now, farewell, until half an hour
from now.

FERDINAND: A thousand, thousand farewells!

(**Miranda** and **Ferdinand** exit, going their separate ways.)

PROSPERO: I am so glad about this! Nothing
on earth could
Give me more pleasure. But I must now
return to
My book of magic. For before suppertime,
I have many things to do.

(**Prospero** exits.)

Scene 2 ⑧

Another part of the island. **Caliban**, **Stephano**, and **Trinculo** enter.

STEPHANO: All right! When the wine is gone, we will drink water, but not a drop before. So cheers, and bottoms up! *(He takes a drink.)* Servant-monster, drink to me!

TRINCULO: Servant-monster! Freak of this island! They say there are only five here—we are three of them. If the other two are as crazy as we are, the country is in trouble!

STEPHANO: My man-monster has drowned his tongue in wine. As for me, the sea cannot drown me! Before I got to the shore, I swam thirty-five leagues, off and on. *(to Caliban)*: You shall be my lieutenant, or my standard-bearer.

TRINCULO: Your lieutenant, if you please. He can hardly even stand!

STEPHANO: Monster, what do you say to that?

CALIBAN: How is my lord? Let me lick your shoe. *(nodding at Trinculo)* I won't serve him. He is not valiant.

TRINCULO: You're lying, you ignorant monster. I am brave enough to push a policeman. You wicked fish! Was any man ever a coward who drank so much wine? How dare you tell such a monstrous lie?

CALIBAN *(to Stephano)*: Listen to how he mocks me! Will you allow it, my lord?

TRINCULO: "Lord," he said! Oh, that a monster should be such a fool!

CALIBAN: Listen, listen, he did it again. Bite him to death, I beg you!

STEPHANO: Trinculo, watch your tongue! The poor monster is one of my subjects, and he shall not suffer embarrassment.

CALIBAN: I thank my noble lord. Will you listen once again to my request?

STEPHANO: Indeed, I would. Kneel, and repeat it. (**Ariel** enters, invisible.)

80

CALIBAN: As I told you before, I'm subject
To a tyrant, a magician. By his cunning,
He has cheated me of this island.

ARIEL: You are lying!

CALIBAN *(thinking Trinculo has spoken)*:
You are lying, you jesting monkey, you!

STEPHANO: Trinculo, if you interrupt his story
again, I'll knock out some of your teeth!

TRINCULO: Why? I said nothing.

STEPHANO: Quiet! No more!
(to Caliban): Go on.

CALIBAN: I say, he got this island through magic.
He took it from me. If your greatness will
Take revenge on him, you can be lord of it,
And I will serve you.

STEPHANO: How can I do this?
Can you bring me to him?

CALIBAN: Yes, my lord. I'll betray him to you
While he's asleep.
Then, you may knock a nail into his head.

ARIEL: You're lying. You cannot do it.

CALIBAN *(thinking Trinculo has spoken again)*: What a fool he is! You idiot!

(to Stephano): I beg your greatness: beat him, And take his bottle away. When that's gone, He'll drink nothing but saltwater, for I'll not Show him where the freshwater streams are.

STEPHANO: Trinculo, watch yourself! Interrupt the monster once more, and I promise, I'll show no mercy. I'll beat you to a pulp!

TRINCULO: Why? What did I do? I did nothing. I'll go farther off.

ARIEL: You lie. . . .

STEPHANO: Do I? Take that! *(hitting Trinculo)* If you liked that, call me a liar again.

TRINCULO: I didn't call you a liar. Have you lost your wits, and your hearing, too? A pox on your bottle! This is what wine and drinking can do. A plague on your monster, and may the devil take your fingers!

CALIBAN: Ha, ha, ha!

STEPHANO *(to Caliban)*: Now, go on with your tale. *(to Trinculo)*: Please stand farther away.

CALIBAN: Beat him soundly. After a little time,
I will beat him, too.

STEPHANO *(to Trinculo, pointing)*: Farther!
(to Caliban): Please, proceed.

CALIBAN: Well, he sleeps every afternoon.
You could smash his brains in then,
Batter his skull with a log, or cut his throat.
  Remember *first* to take his books.
Without them, he's a nobody like me,
Without a single spirit to command.
They all hate him as much as I do.
Just burn his books. But what is most worth
Thinking about is the beauty of his daughter.
He himself says she has no equal.
  I have seen only two women—
My mother Sycorax and her—
But this daughter far outshines Sycorax,
As the greatest outshines the least.

STEPHANO: Is she really that beautiful?

CALIBAN: Yes, lord, and she'll be good in bed,
I guarantee, and give you many fine children.

STEPHANO: Monster, I will kill this man. His
daughter and I will be king and queen—

God save Our Graces! And Trinculo and
you will be viceroys. Do you like the
plot, Trinculo?

TRINCULO: Excellent!

STEPHANO: Give me your hand. I am sorry I
beat you. But please watch what you say.

CALIBAN: Within half an hour, he'll be asleep.
Will you destroy him then?

STEPHANO: Yes, on my honor.

ARIEL *(aside)*: I'll tell my master this.

CALIBAN: I'm so pleased. Shall we sing the song
You taught me a while ago?

STEPHANO: For you, monster, I will do
anything, anything. Come on, Trinculo,
let's sing.
(singing) Mock 'em and sock 'em
And sock 'em and mock 'em!
Thought is free—

(Ariel plays the tune on a drum and a pipe. The
singers stop and listen in surprise.)

STEPHANO: What's all this?

TRINCULO *(frightened)*: That is our song, played by the invisible man!

STEPHANO: If you are a man, show yourself as you are. If you're a devil, choose the shape you like!

TRINCULO *(kneeling)*: Oh, forgive me my sins!

STEPHANO *(crossing himself)*: Mercy on us!

CALIBAN: Are you afraid?

STEPHANO *(trembling)*: No, monster, not I.

CALIBAN: Don't be. The island is full of noises, Sounds that give delight and don't hurt.

STEPHANO: This will be a great kingdom for me. I'll have free music every day!

CALIBAN: When Prospero is destroyed . . .

STEPHANO: That will be soon.

TRINCULO: The sound is going away. Let's follow it, and after that do our work.

STEPHANO: Lead on, monster. We'll follow you. I wish I could see this drummer. He lays it on.

TRINCULO: I will follow you, Stephano.

(**All** exit.)

Scene ❸ 🎧

Another part of the island. **Alonso, Sebastian, Antonio, Gonzalo, Adrian, Francisco,** and **others** enter.

GONZALO: To be sure, I can go no farther, sir.
If you don't mind, I must rest!

ALONSO: Old lord, I can't blame you.
I myself am weary. Sit down, and rest.
Here I will give up hope of finding my son.
Alas, he is drowned, and the sea mocks
Our vain search on land. Well, let him go.

ALONSO *(aside to Sebastian):* I'm glad that he's
Given up hope. Now, don't forget our plans.

SEBASTIAN *(to Antonio):* We'll take the next
opportunity.

ALONSO *(to Sebastian):* Let it be tonight.
They are so tired from traveling they won't
Be as watchful as when they were fresh.

SEBASTIAN *(to Antonio):* Tonight, then.

(Solemn music is heard. **Prospero** enters, invisible.
Spirits bring in a banquet and dance around it,
inviting the king and his party to eat. Then they leave.)

ALONSO: What music is this? Good friends,
listen!

GONZALO: Marvelous sweet music!

ALONSO: What were they?

SEBASTIAN: A living puppet show! Remarkable!

GONZALO: If I reported this now in Naples,
Would they believe me?

ALONSO: I can't help but marvel at how these
Strange spirits communicate without words.

PROSPERO *(aside):* Hold your praise until later.

FRANCISCO: They've vanished strangely!

SEBASTIAN: No matter. They've left this

Banquet behind—and we have appetites.

(to the king) Would you like to try it?

ALONSO: Not I!

GONZALO: I don't think it will harm us.

ALONSO: All right. I will eat.

If it's my last meal, no matter, since I feel

The best part of my life is past.

(Thunder and lightning. **Ariel** enters, looking like the fabled Harpy—a monster with a woman's head and body, and a bird's wings and claws. He claps his wings over the table and the food vanishes.)

ARIEL: You are three men of sin. Fate

Has made the ever-hungry sea belch you up

On this deserted island—you of all men

Being the most unfit to live.

(Alonso and the others draw their swords.)

You fools! I and my fellows are the elements

Of which your swords are made!

You might as well slash at the loud winds

Or stab at the sea as try to hurt

The smallest feather in my plumage!

My fellow spirits are equally strong.

You cannot harm them. But remember—
For this is the reason for my visit to you—
That you three from Milan did overthrow
Good Prospero and expose him and his
Innocent child to the mercy of the sea.

For this foul deed, the gods have stirred up
The seas, the shores, and all the creatures
Against you. They have taken your son away
From you, Alonso. Through me they
Sentence you to lingering suffering
  (Worse than any quick death),
  For the rest of your life.

To guard yourself from their further anger,

There is no alternative but heartfelt sorrow

And a blameless life from now on.

(**Ariel** vanishes in a clap of thunder. Then, to soft music, the **Spirits** return and dance mockingly as they carry out the table.)

PROSPERO: You've acted the role of Harpy

Very well, my Ariel. You did everything

I asked.

So also have my lesser servants done well.

All my spells have worked. My enemies are

Totally confused and now in my power.

I'll leave them like this, while I visit young

Ferdinand, whom they suppose is drowned,

And his—and my—beloved girl.

(**Prospero** exits.)

GONZALO *(to Alonso)*: What are you staring at?

ALONSO: This is monstrous! I thought the waves

And the winds spoke and told me of my sin.

I heard the thunder say the name of

Prospero.

Because of my guilt, my son lies in the ooze
Of the ocean floor. I'll seek him there,
And join him in the mud.

(**Alonso** exits, sorrowfully.)

SEBASTIAN *(defiantly)*: One fiend at a time—
I'll fight whole legions of them!

ANTONIO: I'll be your second.

(**Sebastian** and **Antonio** exit.)

GONZALO: All three of them are desperate.
Their great guilt, like a slow poison,
Now begins to bite their spirits. I beg you
More athletic men to follow them quickly.
Stop them from what this madness
May now provoke them to do.

ADRIAN *(to the others)*: After them, quick!

(**All** exit, running.)

ACT 4

Summary

普洛斯帕羅要求愛麗兒與其他的精靈
為米蘭達與菲迪南獻上一齣劇,為這
對年輕的愛侶的訂婚獻上祝福。但很快普洛斯帕羅想起卡
列班等人正密謀想要害他,於是他為先去處理卡列班而倉
促結束了這場劇。

他對愛麗兒下令,以他的衣服作餌設了一個局。當斯蒂芬
諾與屈林鳩羅看到這些被愛麗兒散落在地、閃閃發光的
衣服時,他們迫不及待的試穿並強迫卡列班將這些衣服
全部帶走,這時精靈們化作獵犬出現了,他們一路追趕著
斯蒂芬諾、屈林鳩羅和卡列班直到將他們趕走。

Scene ❶ 🎧

In front of Prospero's cave. **Prospero**, **Ferdinand**, and **Miranda** enter.

PROSPERO: If I have punished you too severely,
　　Your reward makes up for it. I have given you
　　A third of my own life—that for which I live.
　　Once again, I give you her hand. All your
　　Discomforts and trials were my way of
　　　testing your love,
　　And you passed the test. Oh, Ferdinand,
　　Do not smile at me for boasting about her.
　　You shall find that she is beyond all praise—
　　It can't keep up with her.

FERDINAND: I know that is true.

PROSPERO: So, as my gift and your own gain,
　　Worthily won, take my daughter. But
　　If you sleep with her before the wedding,
　　Your union will not be blessed by heaven, and
　　Hatred and conflict shall ruin your union.
　　Take heed, then, until your wedding day.

FERDINAND: As I hope for quiet days, a family,
　　And long life with enduring love, nothing

Will melt my honor into lust. It would spoil
The joy of our wedding day, when I'll think
Time has stopped and night will never come.

PROSPERO: Well said. Sit and talk with her.
She is yours. *(calling)* Now, Ariel!

(**Ariel** enters.)

ARIEL: What does my powerful master wish?

PROSPERO: You and your assistants performed
Your last service very well. I want you to
Do another trick. Go get your assistants.
I must let this young couple see more
Of my magic art. I promised them, and
They expect it from me.

ARIEL: Right now?

PROSPERO: Yes, in the twinkling of an eye.

ARIEL: Before you can take two breaths,
They will be here. Do you love me, master?

PROSPERO: Dearly, my delicate Ariel. Don't come
Until you hear me call.

ARIEL: I understand.

(**Ariel** exits.)

PROSPERO *(to Ferdinand)*: Now, keep your word. Control your passions, or else you can say Good night to your vow.

FERDINAND: I assure you, sir, that my loved one's Snow-white purity cools the heat of my desire.

PROSPERO: Good. Now come, Ariel. Bring your helpers. Rather than too few performers, Let's have too many! Come now! Quickly! No talking! Eyes open! Silence!

(Soft music plays. The spirits perform a scene. The first spirit appears as Iris, goddess of the rainbow and messenger of the gods. Iris addresses Ceres, goddess of agriculture.)

IRIS: Ceres, generous lady, who makes grow
    The wheat, rye, barley, and oats that we
      sow—
    Your grassy mountains feed the hungry sheep.
    Your meadows yield the food for their keep.
    Your riverbanks with flowers are dressed
    Watered by rainy April at your request.
    The queen of the sky,
    Whose rainbow messenger am I,
    Begs you leave by your royal grace,
    And come to this very place.
    Join in our fun—do not hesitate!
    Come quickly, and help us celebrate!

(**Ceres** enters, played by Ariel.)

CERES: Hail, many-colored messenger,
    Who pleases Juno, wife of Jupiter!
    Tell me now, why has your queen
    Called me here, to this short-grassed
      green?

IRIS: A contract of true love to celebrate,
    And some gift—something to donate
    To the blessed lovers.

CERES: Tell me, heavenly rainbow,
Is Venus, or her son Cupid, do you know,
Still waiting on the queen? Since the sad day
They helped dark Pluto take my daughter
away,
I've sworn to avoid their evil company.

IRIS: Don't be afraid of her society.
I met her in the clouds with her son.
What they thought they had done
Was this: A spell on the couple they'd placed,
To get them to break their vow to be chaste,
But it didn't work.
The gods schemed in vain.
The hot-headed Venus has gone home again.
Her spoiled son, Cupid, has broken his
arrows,
To shoot no more, but play with sparrows,
And behave like a boy again.

CERES: Highest queen of state,
Great Juno comes. I know her by her gait.

(**Juno** enters.)

ACT 4
SCENE
1

JUNO: How is my bountiful sister? Go with me
  To bless these two, so they may
    prosperous be,
  And honored in their children.
  (singing)
  Honor, riches, marriage blessing,
  Long life, and wealth increasing,
  Hourly joys be always upon you!
  Juno sings her blessings on you.

CERES *(singing):* *Good crops and harvests plenty,*
  Barns and haylofts, never empty.
  Vines, with clustering bunches growing,
  Plants, with heavy burdens bowing.
  Spring comes to you at the farthest,
  At the very end of harvest.
  Scarcity and want shall shun you.
  Ceres' blessing so is on you.

FERDINAND: This is a most majestic vision.
  Its theme of harmony is charming. Am I
    right
  To think that these are spirits?

PROSPERO *(nodding):* Spirits, which my art has
  Called upon to do my bidding.

FERDINAND: Let me live here forever.

A father-in-law so wonderful and wise

Makes of this place a paradise.

(Juno and Ceres whisper and send Iris away to perform a task.)

PROSPERO: Ssh, now! Silence! Juno and Ceres

Are whispering. There's more to come.

IRIS: You nymphs, or Naiads, of winding brooks,

With your reedy crowns and harmless looks,

Leave your rippling streams. To this green land

Answer the summons—it's Juno's command.

Come, mild nymphs, and help to celebrate

A contract of true love. Do not be late.

(Several **nymphs** enter.)

You sunburned reapers of August weary,

Come in from the fields, and be merry.

Make a holiday. Your rye-straw hats put on,

And dance with these nymphs, every one.

(Several **reapers**, finely dressed, enter. They join with the nymphs in a graceful dance. Toward the end, Prospero gives a start and speaks. The **dancers** sadly vanish, while strange, hollow, and confused noises are heard.)

PROSPERO *(aside)*: I had forgotten the foul plot

Of that beast, Caliban, and his fellow

  plotters

Against my life. They'll be here any minute.

(to the spirits): Well done! Begone! No more!

FERDINAND *(to Miranda)*: This is strange.

Your father's worked up about something.

MIRANDA: Never until this day have I seen

Him touched with anger, so out of sorts.

PROSPERO *(seeing that Ferdinand is upset)*:

My son, you look worried and dismayed.

Be cheerful, sir. Our entertainment has

  ended.

Our actors were all spirits, as I told you.

They are melted into air, into thin air.

And just as this vision was an illusion,

So tall towers, gorgeous palaces, holy
temples,

And the earth itself—
indeed, all who live on it—

Shall dissolve. Just as this performance
faded,

So not even a cloud will be left behind.

We are such stuff as dreams are made of,

And our little life is rounded off with a
sleep.

Sir, I am angry. Bear with my weakness,

My old brain is troubled.

Do not be disturbed

By my weakness. If you please,
retire to my cave

And rest there for a while. I'll take a walk

To still my unsettled mind.

FERDINAND AND MIRANDA: May you find peace.

(**Ferdinand** and **Miranda** exit.)

PROSPERO: I summon you with a thought.

Thank you, Ariel! Come!

(**Ariel** enters.)

ARIEL: I'm tuned in to your thoughts.

What is your pleasure?

PROSPERO: We must prepare to meet Caliban.

ARIEL: Yes, my master. When I acted the part

Of Ceres, I thought of telling you about it,

But I was afraid it might anger you.

PROSPERO: Tell me again—where did you leave

those rogues?

ARIEL: They were red-hot with drinking,

So full of courage that they struck the air

For breathing in their faces and beat the
  ground
For kissing their feet! Yet they were always
Moving toward here. Then I beat my
  drum and, like unbroken colts,
They pricked up their ears,
Raised their eyes, and lifted up their noses
As they smelled the music. So I put a spell
On their ears and, like calves,
  they followed me
Through sharp thorny bushes that cut
  their skin.
At last I left them in the filthy pool
Near your cave. They are there, dancing about
Up to their chins, making the lake stink
More than their feet.

PROSPERO: Well done, Ariel! Remain invisible
A while longer. Go and get trivial items
From my house, and bring them here as bait
To catch these thieves.

ARIEL: I go, I go.

(**Ariel** exits.)

PROSPERO *(talking about Caliban)*: A devil,
  A born devil, whose nature will never change.
  All the pains I've taken to help him are lost,
  All lost, quite lost. As his body grows uglier
  With age, so does his mind.

(**Ariel** enters, carrying glittering clothes and several other items.)

  Come, hang them on this line.

(Both invisible, they spread them out and step back **Caliban**, **Stephano**, and **Trinculo** enter, all wet.)

CALIBAN: Please, walk softly, so that even a
  Blind mole may not hear a footstep.
  We are now near his cave.

STEPHANO: Monster, your fairy, whom you said
  Is a harmless spirit, has done little more
  Than play the fool with us.

CALIBAN: My lord, be patient with me.
  The prize I'll bring you will blot out this
    mishap.
  So speak softly. All's as quiet as midnight.

TRINCULO: But to lose our bottles in the pool—

STEPHANO: It's not only a disgrace and
  A dishonor, monster, but a great loss!

TRINCULO: It's even worse than getting wet.
Yet this is your "harmless" fairy, monster!

STEPHANO: I'll get my bottle back,
Even if I drown for my labor!

CALIBAN: Please, my king, be quiet. Look here.
This is the mouth of the cave. Enter quietly.
Do that good deed of mischief that will
make this island yours forever,
And I—your Caliban—
Forever your foot-licker.

STEPHANO: Give me your hand.
I begin to have bloody thoughts.

TRINCULO *(noticing the fancy clothes hanging)*:
Oh, lord! Oh, worthy Stephano!
Look at the wardrobe that is here for you.

CALIBAN: Leave it alone, you fool. It is but trash.

TRINCULO *(trying on a robe)*: Oh, no, monster!
We know what belongs in a thrift shop!
(parading around) Oh, King Stephano!

STEPHANO: Take off that robe, Trinculo. I want it!

TRINCULO *(bowing)*: Your grace shall have it.
(He hands it over.)

CALIBAN: May the fool drop dead! Why are you
Drooling over these clothes? Leave them
alone,
And do the murder first. If he wakes up,
He'll pinch us from head to toe and
torture us.
He might even turn us into wild geese
Or into apes with low foreheads!

STEPHANO: Monster, help us carry these clothes,
Or I'll turn you out of my kingdom. Here,
Carry these! *(They pile clothes on Caliban.)*

TRINCULO: And this.

STEPHANO: Yes, and this.

(Hunting noises are heard. **Spirits** enter, disguised as dogs. Encouraged by Prospero and Ariel, they chase Stephano, Trinculo, and Caliban.)

PROSPERO: Hey, Mountain, hey!

ARIEL: Silver! There it goes, Silver!

PROSPERO: Fury, Fury! There, Tyrant, there!

(**Stephano**, **Trinculo**, and **Caliban** are chased away.)

PROSPERO *(calling after the dogs)*: Go,
   Tell my goblins to grind their joints with
      pain,
   Tighten their muscles with cramps,
   And pinch their skin until they're more
      spotted
   Than panthers or leopards!

ARIEL: Listen to them roar!

PROSPERO: Let them be hunted well. At this
      hour,
   All of my enemies are at my mercy.
   Soon my work shall end, and you
   Shall be as free as the air. For just a
      little longer,
   Follow my instructions and serve me.

(**Prospero** and **Ariel** exit.)

ACT 5

Summary

普洛斯帕羅讓愛麗兒去請來船難的生
還者與還待在船上的水手們，船在暴風雨中並沒有損壞，而
是停泊在附近一處小海灣。

普洛斯帕羅與阿隆佐終於面對面了，他原諒了阿隆佐作的
一切，但他要求要回他的爵位和封地；當普洛斯帕羅讓阿
隆佐知道他的兒子菲迪南並沒有死時，阿隆佐大喜過望。

而初次見到其他人的米蘭達則讚嘆著人類的美麗；普洛斯
帕羅與阿隆佐和解了，並期待著他們孩子們的婚姻。至於
愛麗兒，普洛斯帕羅終究讓他獲得了自由。

Scene 1 🎧

A little later, in front of Prospero's cave. **Prospero** enters, wearing his magic robes, followed by **Ariel**.

PROSPERO: Now my plan is coming together.
My spells are working, my spirits obey,
And everything is on schedule. What is
the time of day?

ARIEL: 6:00, when you said our work would end.

PROSPERO: I did say that,
When I first raised the tempest. Tell me,
spirit,
How are the king and his followers?

ARIEL: Kept together, just as you left them.
They're prisoners in the grove near your cave.
They can't budge until you release them.
The king, his brother, and your brother
Are distressed. The rest mourn over them,
Full of sorrow and dismay. Most affected is
The one you call "the good old lord
Gonzalo."
His tears run down his beard like winter rain
From a thatched roof. Your spell is so strong

That if you now saw them,
Your feelings would be touched.

PROSPERO: Do you think so, spirit?

ARIEL: Mine would be, sir, if I were human.

PROSPERO: So shall mine. If you, mere air,
Can feel sympathy for them, then surely I can.
Go release them, Ariel. I'll break my spells.
I'll restore their senses,
And they will be themselves once again.

ARIEL: I'll fetch them, sir.

(**Ariel** exits.)

PROSPERO: You elves of hills, brooks, and groves!
And you light-footed spirits who chase the sea
When it ebbs, only to run away
   when it flows back!
You fairies who make rings on the village green
At midnight, so sour that sheep will not
   chew it!
With your aid, lesser spirits though you are,
I have dimmed the noonday sun,
Called forth violent winds, and made the
Green sea and the blue sky wage roaring war.
I have split stout oaks with thunderbolts.

Graves have opened at my command, and
Their awakened sleepers have come forth.
But this rough magic I now give up.
When I have requested some heavenly
   music—
Which I do now—to charm their senses,
I'll break my wand in two. Then I'll bury it
In the earth to the proper depth. After that,
I'll drown my magician's book in the deepest
Part of the ocean.

(Solemn music is played. **Ariel** enters, followed by
Alonso, who is gesturing frantically, like a man who
has lost his mind. **Gonzalo** is looking after him.
Sebastian and **Antonio** also seem demented and are
cared for by **Adrian** and **Francisco**. They all enter
Prospero's magic circle and stand there, spellbound.
Prospero speaks to them.)

Let solemn music, the best comforter
To a troubled mind, cure your brains
That lie so useless in your skulls!
Stand there, for you are under a spell.
   Holy Gonzalo, honorable man,
My eyes shed tears of sympathy for you.
The charm quickly dissolves. Just as the
Morning melts the darkness of the night,

So your rising senses clear the ignorance
That clouds your clearer reason.
Oh, good Gonzalo, my true savior,
   I will reward you for your services,
Both in word and in deed. Alonso,
You used me and my daughter most cruelly.
Your brother helped you do so.
Your conscience bothers you now,
Sebastian!
(to Antonio): You, my brother,
My own flesh and blood, you let ambition
Come between us. Yet I do forgive you,
Unnatural though you are.

(Gonzalo, Alonso, Sebastian, and Antonio are
gradually coming out of the spell.)

Their understanding is beginning to flood
   back.
None of them can see me now,
Nor would they know me if they could.
Ariel, fetch me the hat and my sword.
I'll remove my robe, and present myself
As the Duke of Milan. Quickly, spirit!
Soon you shall be free.

(Ariel sings as he helps Prospero dress.)

ARIEL: *Where the bee sucks, there suck I,*
On a primrose petal, I lie.
There I sleep when owls cry,
And on the bat's back I do fly
After summer, merrily.
Merrily, merrily shall I live now,
Under the blossom that hangs on the bough.

PROSPERO: That's my dainty Ariel! I will miss
You, but you shall have your freedom.

(He arranges his uniform to look his best.)

ACT 5
SCENE
1

So, so, so.
(to Ariel again): Go to the king's ship, invisibly.
Find the sailors asleep below deck.
When the captain and the boatswain
Are awake, make them come here.
Go quickly, if you please!

ARIEL: I'll streak through the air, and return
Before your pulse can beat twice.

(**Ariel** exits.)

GONZALO: This place is all torment, trouble,
Wonder, and amazement.

113

May some heavenly power guide us
Out of this fearful country!

PROSPERO *(confronting Alonso)*: Behold, King,
The wronged Duke of Milan—Prospero!
To prove to you that a living prince,
     and not a spirit
Does now speak to you,
     I embrace your body.
(He holds Alonso to him.) I bid you welcome.

ALONSO: Whether you are Prospero or not,
I do not know. Your pulse beats like a man's.
Since seeing you, the strange madness
     I've been under
Seems to have ended. If this is real,
It's part of a very strange story.
I will no longer demand tribute money.
I beg you to pardon me for my wrongs.
But how can Prospero still be living,
     and be *here*?

PROSPERO *(turning to Gonzalo)*: First,
Noble friend, let me embrace your old self,
Whose honor cannot be measured or limited
     in any way.

GONZALO *(dazed)*: I have no idea
  Whether this is really happening or not.

PROSPERO: You are still under the island's spell.
  It stops you from believing in reality.
  Welcome, my friends, one and all.
  (aside to Sebastian and Antonio): But you,
  My fine pair of lords, if I felt like it,
  I could expose you to the king as traitors.
    But for now, I will tell no tales.

SEBASTIAN *(aside)*: It's the devil speaking!

PROSPERO: No! *(to Antonio)*: As for you,
  You wicked man, to call you "brother"
  Would infect my mouth. But I forgive you.
  I require my dukedom from you, which
  You have no choice but to return.

ALONSO: If you are Prospero, tell us how you
  Were saved and how you met us here—
  Where three hours ago we were shipwrecked
  And where I have lost my dear son Ferdinand.

PROSPERO: I am sorry about that, sir. I suspect
  you have not sought the help of patience.

ALONSO: The loss is irreparable. Patience
  cannot cure it.

115

PROSPERO: I had a loss like yours.

I asked her help, and I now rest content.

ALONSO: You—a similar loss?

PROSPERO: As great to me as yours is to you.

I have lost my daughter.

(He means, of course, that she is engaged to be married.)

ALONSO: A daughter? Oh, heavens!

Oh, if only they were both living in Naples,

As the king and queen there!

When did you lose your daughter?

PROSPERO: In this last tempest.

(He changes the subject.) I see these lords

Are astonished at this meeting. They hardly

Believe that their eyes tell them the truth.

But know for certain that I am Prospero,

The very duke who was expelled from Milan,

And who landed on this very shore

Where you were shipwrecked. That's enough

For now, for it is a long story.

Welcome, sir. This cave is my court.

Here, I have few servants and no subjects.

Please look around inside. Since you have

returned my dukedom, I will pay you back

With something just as good. It will make you

As happy as my dukedom makes me.

(Prospero reveals Ferdinand and Miranda, playing chess inside the cave.)

ALONSO: If this is an illusion of the island,

I will have lost my dear son twice!

SEBASTIAN: A miracle from on high!

FERDINAND *(astonished to see Alonso alive)*: Though

the seas threaten, they are merciful.

I have cursed them without cause.

ACT 5

SCENE 1

ALONSO: May the blessings of a happy father

Protect you always. How did you get here?

MIRANDA: Oh, wonder!

How many fine people there are here!

How lovely mankind is! Oh, brave new world

That has such people in it!

PROSPERO: It's new to you.

ALONSO *(to Ferdinand)*: Who is this maid
With whom you were playing chess? You
Cannot have known her for more than
three hours.
Is she the goddess that separated us
And brought us back together?

FERDINAND: Sir, she is mortal. By God's grace,
She's mine. I chose her when I couldn't ask
My father for advice—nor thought I had one.
She is daughter to this famous Duke of Milan
Of whom I had often heard, but never seen.
From him I have received a second life.
And this lady makes him a second father
to me.

ALONSO: And I am hers.
But, how odd it will sound
For me to ask my child for forgiveness!

PROSPERO: Stop there, sir. Let's not bring up
Memories of past sorrows.

GONZALO: I have wept inside, or I'd have spoken
Before this. Look down, you gods,
And on this couple drop a blessed crown.

ALONSO: Amen to that, Gonzalo!

GONZALO: Was the Duke of Milan expelled
from Milan so his grandson could be
King of Naples?
Oh, rejoice, and write it with gold on granite:
In one voyage Claribel found her husband
In Tunis, and her brother Ferdinand
Found a wife when he himself was lost.
Prospero found his dukedom on a poor
island,
And all of us have found ourselves.

ALONSO: Give me your hands.
Let grief and sorrow fill the heart of anyone
Who does not wish you joy!

GONZALO: So be it! Amen!

(**Ariel** enters, with the **captain** and the **boatswain**
following after him in amazement.)

Oh, look, sir, here are more of us!
I predicted that if a gallows were on land,
That fellow could not drown. Silent now,
are you? You swore enough on board!
What's the news?

BOATSWAIN: The best news is that we have
Safely found our king and company.

The next is that our ship—
Which only three hours ago was split—
Is in one piece, shipshape, and well-rigged!

ARIEL *(aside to Prospero)*: Sir, I did all of this
Since I last left you.

PROSPERO *(aside to Ariel)*: My clever spirit!

ALONSO: Things go from strange to stranger.
Say, how did you get here?

BOATSWAIN: If I thought, sir, that I were awake,
I'd try to tell you. We were sound asleep,
And—just how, we don't know—stuck
    below decks.
Then, only now, various strange noises
Of roaring, shrieking, howling, jangling
    chains, and other sounds,
All horrible, awakened us.
Suddenly, we were free! Then we saw
Our royal, good, and gallant ship.
Our captain jumped for joy to
    see her. Then suddenly,
As if in a dream, we were taken from
The rest of the crew and brought here,
    dazed.

ARIEL *(to Prospero):* Was it well-done?

PROSPERO *(to Ariel):* Perfectly! You shall be free.

ALONSO: Some oracle must explain this to us.

PROSPERO: Sir, don't trouble your mind with
Trying to figure out this business.
At our convenience, which shall be soon,
I'll explain it to you. Until then, be cheerful,
And think of everything as good. Come,
faithful spirit,
Set Caliban and his companions free.
It's time to undo the spell.

ACT 5
SCENE
1

(**Ariel** exits. Prospero turns to Alonso.)

How do you feel, my gracious sir?
There are still a few lads missing.

(**Ariel** returns, leading in **Caliban**, **Stephano**, and
Trinculo, still wearing their stolen clothing.)

STEPHANO *(still drunk, and getting his thoughts mixed
up):* Every man help all the rest, and let
no man take care of himself. It's all a
matter of luck! Courage, monster!

TRINCULO: If my eyes tell the truth, here's a
good sight!

CALIBAN *(admiring everyone)*: Oh, the devil!
These are brave spirits indeed! How fine
my master looks! I am afraid he will
punish me.

SEBASTIAN: Ha, ha! What are these things,
Antonio? Will money buy them?

ANTONIO: Probably. *(eyeing Caliban)* One is
Quite strange, and no doubt could
easily be bought.

PROSPERO: Look at what these men are wearing,
My lords. Then judge if they are honest.
(pointing to Caliban) This ugly knave,
His mother was a witch, so strong she
Could control the moon and tides.
These three have stolen from me, and this
Monster had plotted with them to kill me.
Two of these fellows are yours, but this thing
Of darkness *(pointing to Caliban)* is mine.

CALIBAN: I shall be pinched to death!

ALONSO: Isn't this Stephano, my drunken
butler?

SEBASTIAN: Clearly, he is drunk now.
Where did he get wine?

ALONSO: And Trinculo is tipsy, too.

Where did they find this strong liquor?

(to Trinculo): How did you get in this pickle?

TRINCULO: I have been in such a pickle since

I last saw you. I am so well-preserved that

No flies will ever land on me!

PROSPERO *(to Caliban)*: Go to my cave,

And take your companions with you.

If you want my pardon, behave yourself.

CALIBAN: I will, sir. I'll be wise from now on

And try to please you. What an idiot I was

To take this drunkard for a god

And worship such a dull fool!

PROSPERO: Off with you now.

ALONSO: Put that stuff back where you found it.

SEBASTIAN: Or, rather, *stole* it.

PROSPERO *(to Alonso)*: Sir, I invite your highness

And your followers to my poor cave.

Where you can rest.

Part of this one night,

I'll spend in talk that will make

the time go quickly.

I'll tell you the story of my life, and the
particular details
Of my stay on this island. In the morning
I will bring you to your ship, and then,
on to Naples.
There I hope to see our loved ones'
wedding
Before I shall retire to Milan, where
Every third thought shall be of my grave.

ALONSO: I long to hear the story of your life,
Which must be a very strange one.

PROSPERO: I will tell you everything,
And I promise you calm seas, favorable
winds,
And a voyage so speedy that you'll catch
Your royal fleet, far off though it is.
(aside to Ariel): These are your orders, my
Ariel.
Then may you be as free as the air, and
fare you well!
(to the company, indicating his cave): If you
please, come and join me now.

(**All** exit.)

Epilogue
Spoken by Prospero

Now my spells are all overthrown,
What strength I have is mine alone.
I am a weak man, now it's true,
I must be detained here by you
Or sent to Naples. Let me not—
Since I have my dukedom got
And pardoned my brother—dwell
On this bare island, by your spell.
Please release me from my bands
With the help of your good hands.
As you from crimes would pardoned be,
Let your applause now set me free.

(**Prospero** exits.)

ACT 5
SCENE 1

中文翻譯·

英文內文 P. 004

背景介紹

遭受弟弟背叛的普洛斯帕羅，失去了米蘭公爵的爵位。過去這十二年來，他一直和如今已經十五歲的女兒米蘭達生活在一座荒島上。普洛斯帕羅嗜書如命，雖然這是他失去爵位的主要原因，但這項興趣卻也同時讓他能夠施展魔法控制這座島嶼。

長相醜陋的卡列班是女巫席考拉克斯的兒子，他不情願地服侍著普洛斯帕羅；而先前被女巫席考拉克斯囚禁在松樹裡的精靈愛麗兒，現在也是普洛斯帕羅的侍從。故事一開始，普洛斯帕羅用魔法引起了一場暴風雨，造成船難，並將他的敵人帶到這座島上。

劇中角色

阿隆佐：那不勒斯王

瑟拜士梯安：阿隆佐之弟

普洛斯帕羅：法定的米蘭公爵

安東尼奧：普洛斯帕羅之弟，現在的米蘭公爵

菲迪南：那不勒斯王之子

貢札羅：正直的老臣

阿特利安與**法朗西斯科**：侍臣

卡列班：醜怪的奴隸

屈林鳩羅：丑角

斯蒂芬諾：愛酗酒的廚師

船長

水手頭目：負責管理水手和裝備的長官

眾水手

米蘭達：普洛斯帕羅之女

愛麗兒：縹緲的精靈

伊麗斯、刻瑞斯、朱諾、寧芙、收割農人：眾精靈

第一幕

●第一場 ──────────────────────── P. 007

一艘船在暴風雨中搖晃顛簸,船長和水手頭目走上甲板。

船長:水手頭目!

水手頭目:在這兒,船長。什麼事?

船長:好傢伙,去和水手們說,叫他們動作快一點,不然我們
就要觸礁了,快一點!

(船長下,吹著哨子。眾水手衝上前,開始拉著船帆。)

水手頭目:用力啊,我的兄弟們!用力拉啊!快點!把桅帆收進
來。聽船長的哨音指揮。(對著暴風雨吶喊:)儘管吹破你的
肺吧!我們的船不會有事的。

(阿隆佐上,伴隨著瑟拜士梯安、安東尼奧、菲迪南、貢札羅、和其
他人。)

阿隆佐:水手頭目,船長人呢?

水手頭目:你沒聽到他的聲音嗎?你擋到路了!待在船艙裡吧,
你們根本是暴風雨派來的幫手!

貢札羅:別這樣,好伙伴,有點耐心。

水手頭目:等海浪有耐心再說吧!(指著大浪)你覺得它在乎你
們是不是國王嗎?回你們的船艙去!安靜點!別擋路!

貢札羅:好先生,你可別忘了是誰在這艘船上。

水手頭目:我當然知道,但是我愛惜自己的生命勝過其他人。
你是大臣,如果你有本事命令這陣風雨停下來,請你趕快
下令;如果沒辦法,那就感謝上天讓你活了那麼久,然後回

到船艙，準備面對接下來的苦難吧！（對其他船客：）別擋路！沒聽到我說的話嗎！

（水手頭目下，大聲喊叫著命令。）

貢札羅：這傢伙給了我很大的安慰，他命中註定要被吊死而非淹死。命運之神啊！請保佑他的絞刑，讓他命運的繩索成為我們的船錨，因為我們的船錨一點也不管用。如果他不是生來註定要受絞刑吊死的話，我們可就有麻煩了。

（阿隆佐和其他人下，水手頭目再次上場。）

水手頭目（對著水手）：桅帆拉下來！快一點！再低一點，再低一點！（甲板之下傳來乘客的大聲叫喊。）喊得這麼大聲，都比外面的暴風大聲啦！（瑟拜士梯安、安東尼奧、和貢札羅再次上場。）怎麼又是你們啊！你們到底要做什麼？乾脆我們放棄一起淹死好不好？你們想要讓船沉了嗎？

瑟拜士梯安：願你窒息而死，你這隻吠叫的狗！

水手頭目：那你來幫忙啊。

安東尼奧：吊死你這隻狗！吊死你這個大嘴巴！我們才沒像你那麼怕被淹死。

貢札羅：我保證他不會被淹死，儘管這艘船沒有堅果殼來得堅固。

水手頭目（對水手）：把帆拉起來！主帆拉起來！往海中開去。轉向！

（眾水手上，他們全身濕透，臉色驚恐。）

水手：一切都完了。祈禱吧！沒有希望了。（眾水手下。）

貢札羅：國王和王子正在禱告，我們趕快加入他們吧，這似乎是唯一的希望了。

（不同的祈禱聲傳來。「憐憫我們！再會，我的妻兒。再見，我的兄弟！天啊！不！船毀了，船毀了！」）

安東尼奧：讓我們和國王一同沉沒吧。

瑟拜士梯安：我們必須和他好好道別。

（安東尼奧和瑟拜士梯安下。）

貢札羅：我願意用眼前的大海換一小塊的不毛之地！就照上帝的旨意行事吧！但我寧可死在陸地上。

（貢札羅下。）

●第二場 P. 011

在一座島上，普洛斯帕羅洞穴前的一處空地。普洛斯帕羅和米蘭達上。

米蘭達：我親愛的父親啊，如果這場暴風雨是你使用魔法所召喚的話，趕快停止吧。天空好像下起燃燒的瀝青，而海浪跳起來切斷這些火焰。唉，看到這些人受苦，我也難過不已！一艘美麗的船，一定載著高貴的人，現在卻被暴風雨撞得四分五裂。人們的慘叫聲真令人心碎，這些可憐的人，應該已經死去了吧！如果我有一絲神力，我會將海沉到地面下，絕不會讓它將這艘美麗的船吞噬，奪去這些可憐人的生命。

普洛斯帕羅：冷靜點，別難過。告訴你自己那顆善良的心，一點傷害都沒有發生。

米蘭達：唉，真是可怕的一天啊！

普洛斯帕羅：沒事的，我親愛的女兒啊，我所做的一切都是為你好。你不知道自己的身分，也不知道我來自何方。你不知道我真實的身分不只是普洛斯帕羅，不僅僅是一個住在簡陋洞穴的卑微父親而已。

米蘭達：我從沒想過我該知道的更多。

普洛斯帕羅：是該讓你知道的時候了，幫我把身上的法袍脫去。

（米蘭達遵照指示，普洛斯帕羅將法袍放在一塊岩石上。）擦乾你的眼淚，安靜聽我說。你看到的船沉入大海的恐怖景象，卻對人類毫無傷害；你聽到了沉入海中的人們的哭喊，但即便是他們的毛髮都不會受到一點傷害。坐下來，是時候讓你知道更多事了。

米蘭達：每當你開始想要告訴我我是誰，便又會突然閉上嘴不肯說，並總是在我提出問題的時候說：「不要再問了，還不是時候。」

普洛斯帕羅：現在時機已經成熟。仔細聽，注意聽。你還記得我們來到這個洞穴之前發生的事嗎？我想你應該不記得，因為當時你才三歲不到。

米蘭達：父親，我當然記得。

普洛斯帕羅：你記得些什麼？我們住的地方？還是記得誰？

米蘭達：這些記憶模糊而遙遠，就好像一場夢。以前是不是有四五個女人照顧我？

普洛斯帕羅：當然，還不止四五個，米蘭達。但是這些怎麼會還在你的腦海中呢？在你的記憶中，你還記得些什麼？如果你還記得以前的事，或許你可以想起當初是如何來到這裡的。

米蘭達：但我記不得了。

普洛斯帕羅：米蘭達，十二年前，你的父親是米蘭公爵，一位權傾一時的國王。

米蘭達：父親，你不是我的父親嗎？

普洛斯帕羅：你的母親是美德的化身，她告訴我你是我的女兒。你的父親是米蘭公爵，他唯一的繼承人是你，一位高貴的公主。

米蘭達：天啊！我們遭受了什麼奸計迫害，流落到這個地方？還是說因為我們做了好事才這樣呢？

普洛斯帕羅：都是，都是，我的乖女兒！如你所說，我們被奸計迫害，但我們也是因為上天的眷顧才會到這裡來。

米蘭達：天啊，父親，一想起我對你所造成的麻煩，我的心就在滴血，這些我卻都不記得了，再多告訴我一些。

普洛斯帕羅：我的弟弟叫做安東尼奧。啊！一個兄弟竟然可以如此邪惡！我對他的愛僅次於對你，我信任他，將王國交給他管理。當時，米蘭是最強的城邦，而我是這個城邦的公爵。我的知識學問無人可及，我耽溺於學問的追求，將國家交給我的弟弟治理，卻和我的王國漸行漸遠。我成天在書房中埋首苦讀，而你那個邪惡的叔叔——你有在聽我說話嗎？

米蘭達：有的，父親，我非常仔細在聽！

普洛斯帕羅：他學會如何對屬下施惠，如何拒絕請求。他學會該拔擢何人，該開除何人。藉此，他得到我的支持者的效忠，他既具有個人影響力，同時獨攬王權，得以對我的王國發號施令。最後，他的茁壯就像一株常春藤，遮住了我王者的樹幹，吸走了我的精髓。你有專心聽嗎？

米蘭達：啊！我的好父親，當然有啊！

普洛斯帕羅：仔細聽好。我荒廢了朝政，專心學問，滋養了我弟弟邪惡的一面。對他無盡的信任，激起了他對我無限的欺騙。他因為我的財富而富有，因為我的信任而壯大。我們互換了角色，他代理朝政，享有特權。他像一個說謊的人開始相信自己的謊言——他才是真的米蘭公爵。日復一日，他的野心慢慢茁壯。你有在聽嗎？

米蘭達：你的故事，父親，足以治癒耳聾的人。

普洛斯帕羅：他想當的是真正的公爵！至於我，可憐的傻子，對我來說我的圖書室已經是一座王國。很快地他開始覺得我無法處理朝政，為了權力，他和那不勒斯王結盟，並同意對他朝貢臣服。他將當時不可一世的米蘭臣服於那不勒斯，這是多麼大的屈辱啊！唉，可憐的米蘭啊！

米蘭達：啊，天啊！

普洛斯帕羅：聽我說完他所締結的條約，和其導致的結果，然後告訴我這是不是一個兄弟應該做的事情。

米蘭達：我如果這樣想，怕是對我高貴的祖母無禮，但是良善的母親的確會生出邪惡的兒子。

普洛斯帕羅：現在說他們所簽訂的條約。這個那不勒斯王一向是我的敵人，他答應了我弟弟的要求，讓我的弟弟對他朝貢稱臣，不知花了多少國庫的錢。作為交換，那不勒斯王將立即驅逐我和我的家人出國，將我的王位交給我的弟弟。然後，叛軍興起，在一個致命的夜晚，安東尼奧打開了米蘭的城門。在死寂的黑暗中，他的黨羽將我，以及哭泣中的你，趕出了米蘭。

米蘭達：唉，真是可悲！我忘了當初是怎麼哭的，但是現在我想再哭一遍，這個故事將淚水帶到了我的眼前。

普洛斯帕羅：再聽我繼續講，很快就會和現在發生的事有所關聯。如果沒有前面這些事情發生，這個故事就一點也不重要。

米蘭達：當時他們為什麼不直接殺了我們？

普洛斯帕羅：好問題，我的好女孩。他們不敢，因為我的人民過於愛戴我，而且他們不敢讓自己的惡行染上鮮血。簡單的說，他們將我們趕上船，將我們帶到海外，丟在另一艘破船上。船上沒有索具、滑車、船帆、船桅，就連老鼠都會逃離這艘船。我們被丟在船上，對著怒吼的大海哭喊，對著輕嘆的狂風嘆息。

米蘭達：唉，我不知道給你帶來了多少麻煩！

普洛斯帕羅：不，你是拯救了我的天使。當我對著大海哭泣、痛苦不堪的時候，你那天使般的美麗笑容救了我。

米蘭達：我們是如何上岸的？

普洛斯帕羅：上天保佑，一位名叫貢札羅的那不勒斯人，給了我們食物和新鮮的水、乾淨的衣服、布匹和許多補給品。高貴且仁慈的他，知道我愛書成癖，也從我的書室裡拿了一些我視如己命的書籍給我。

米蘭達：我真希望有朝一日能見這位恩人一面。

普洛斯帕羅：聽完最後一段故事。我們到了這座島上，作為你的老師，我給了你良好的教育，你得到了比其他的公主更多的知識，因為她們將時間花在無謂的事物上，而且她們的教師也不會像我對你如此般的關心照顧。

米蘭達：我真的很感謝你！但是，父親──這件事還是縈繞在我心中──為什麼你要興起這場暴風雨呢？

普洛斯帕羅：我現在告訴你。因緣際會，命運之神現在站在我這一邊，將我的仇家帶到這座島上；我的預感還告訴我，幸運之星現在正在我頭上閃爍著，我必須把握時機，機不可失，失不再來，現在不要再問問題了。（*他將手輕輕在她眼前移過。*）你想睡了，這樣的感覺很好，就順服這樣的感覺吧，我知道你沒有選擇。（*米蘭達睡著。*）現身吧，我的僕人，我已準備好了。來吧，我的愛麗兒。

（*精靈愛麗兒上。*）

愛麗兒：讚美偉大的主人！讚美博學的主人！我來聽候你的指令了，不論你要我上山、下海、跳入火中、漫步雲海，愛麗兒和他的精靈伙伴隨時等候差遣。

普洛斯帕羅：精靈，你有按照我的指示，引起一場暴風雨嗎？

愛麗兒：每個細節都做了，我跳上了國王的船，在船頭、甲板下、甲板上、每個船艙，我都引起了人們的驚恐。我化身成火焰，分佈在船的每個角落，最後合而為一。震雷作響之前的閃電，都沒有我的火焰頻繁炫目。雷電的炸響聲像是在包圍偉大的海神尼普頓（**編注：波賽頓**），讓他無畏的海浪顫抖。

普洛斯帕羅：勇敢的精靈！有誰可以在這場騷動中不失去理智嗎？

愛麗兒：船上的每個人都發瘋了，驚慌失措。除了水手之外，其他人都離開了燃燒中的船隻，跳入了大海。國王的兒子菲迪南是第一個跳下去的，他的頭髮像海草般聳立，哭喊著：「地獄空了，所有的魔鬼都在這裡了！」

普洛斯帕羅：做的真好，我的精靈！但船就在岸邊吧？

愛麗兒：很接近的，我的主人。

普洛斯帕羅：他們都平安無事吧，愛麗兒？

愛麗兒：毫髮無傷，如你所吩咐的，我將他們分散在這座島的
　　　　不同地方。國王的兒子是我讓他自個兒上岸，我將他帶到
　　　　一個偏僻的角落，留他自己在那裡獨自嘆息，他坐在地上，
　　　　手臂交疊得像是一個悲傷的死結。（他示範動作。）

普洛斯帕羅：你如何處置那艘船、水手、還有其他的船隻？

愛麗兒：國王的船隻平安地停靠在港口，它在一處深灣，就是
　　　　有一次你半夜叫我去採百慕達魔術露水的那個地方。我把
　　　　水手拖到甲板下的船艙，對他們施了睡眠之術，因為他們需
　　　　要休息。其他的船隻先前被我分開了，現在聚集在地中海。
　　　　他們親眼目睹國王遇到船難，傷心地以為國王淹死了，準備
　　　　回那不勒斯去。

普洛斯帕羅：你做得很好，如我所吩咐。但是，愛麗兒，你還
　　　　有其他的事要辦。現在是什麼時候了？

愛麗兒：已經過中午了。

普洛斯帕羅：至少兩點了，從現在到晚上六點，我們得好好地
　　　　運用這段時間。

愛麗兒：還有其他的事要做？既然你要我做這麼多事，讓我提
　　　　醒你一下，你答應過我的事，到現在都還沒有實現。

普洛斯帕羅：什麼？你不高興了嗎？你還能要求什麼？

愛麗兒：我的自由。

普洛斯帕羅：在期限之前嗎？我現在不想聽！

愛麗兒：恕我直言，別忘了我為你所做的一切，我從來沒有對
　　　　你撒過謊，也從來沒有犯過錯誤，任勞任怨，毫無怨言，你
　　　　答應過我要提早一年讓我自由的。

普洛斯帕羅：你忘了我是把你從何等苦難中拯救出來的嗎？

愛麗兒：沒有。

普洛斯帕羅：你一定是忘了！行走在海洋之上、奔跑在北極的寒風中、當地面結出一層層的厚冰時，在深海中執行我的命令，現在你開始覺得這一切麻煩了。

愛麗兒：主人，我沒有。

普洛斯帕羅：你說謊，你這個邪惡的東西！你難道忘了那個隨著年紀和憎恨增長，而愈發駝背的邪惡女巫席考拉克斯嗎？你難道不記得她了嗎？

愛麗兒：主人，我還記得。

普洛斯帕羅：你忘記了！不然你告訴我她出生在哪裡？說啊。回答我！

愛麗兒：主人，她出生於阿爾及厄。

普洛斯帕羅：喔，是這樣的嗎？每個月我都要提醒你一次你所遺忘的一切遭遇。這個邪惡的女巫席考拉克斯，因為無數不堪入耳的惡行和施行可怕的巫術，被驅除出阿爾及厄，卻因為一件事而沒有被處死，沒有錯吧？

愛麗兒：是的，主人。

普洛斯帕羅：這個藍眼的魔女被帶到這座島上時懷有身孕。你這個自稱是我的「奴隸」的人，當初是她的僕人。因為你的心思纖細，拒絕執行她那令人作噁的命令。因為這樣的緣故，她發狂大怒，將你關在劈開的松樹裡頭。在其他惡靈的協助之下，她讓你在裡面受了最大的苦達十二年之久。後來她死了，你仍關在樹中，痛苦呻吟的速度像水車打水一樣快速。當時，島上只有兩個人——你，還有那個滿臉雀斑的女巫之子。

愛麗兒：是的，那是卡列班，女巫之子。

普洛斯帕羅：那個愚蠢之徒！我說的就是他：他現在是我的僕人。你很清楚當時所受的痛苦，你的呻吟讓狼群嚎叫，觸動怒熊的心扉。這一切的折磨，連席考拉克斯都無法幫你解脫。是我來到這座島時，聽到了你的慘叫聲，用我的魔法打開了松樹的禁錮，並放你出來。

愛麗兒：我感謝你，主人。

普洛斯帕羅：如果你再抱怨，我就會劈開橡樹，將你鎖在樹結當中，你就準備在裡面哀嚎度過十二個冬天吧！

愛麗兒：原諒我，主人！我會聽話，服從你的命令。

普洛斯帕羅：最好如此，兩天後我就會讓你獲得自由。

愛麗兒：這真是我高貴的主人啊！我該做什麼事？趕快告訴我，你要我做什麼？

普洛斯帕羅：變成一個只有我能看到的海仙女。去，去變身，變完後再回來。現在就去，照我的話做。

（愛麗兒下。普洛斯帕羅轉向沉睡中的米蘭達。）

普洛斯帕羅：醒來吧，我的甜心，醒來。你睡得真熟，醒來吧。

米蘭達：你的故事讓我昏昏欲睡。

普洛斯帕羅：醒來吧，跟我過來。我們要去找卡列班，那個沒給過我們好臉色看的奴隸。

（他轉向附近的一座洞穴的入口。）

米蘭達：他是惡棍，我不想看到他！

普洛斯帕羅：即便如此，我們得靠他幫我們搬木材、生火、做工。（往洞穴裡頭喊叫）喂，我的奴隸！卡列班！你這個蠢貨，回答我！

卡列班（從洞穴裡面）：裡面的木材已經夠用了。

普洛斯帕羅：我要你出來！你這隻烏龜！還要我等多久？（愛麗兒上，已經化身為海仙女。）真是美麗！我聰明的愛麗兒，我有話對你說。（和愛麗兒竊竊私語。）

愛麗兒：我的主人，沒問題。

（愛麗兒下。）

普洛斯帕羅（對卡列班）：你這個包藏禍心的奴隸，惡魔和女巫所生的孽種，快出來！

（卡列班上，他是一個醜陋的怪物。）

卡列班：但願腐爛沼澤的毒露滴在你們兩個身上！但願熱風吹向你們，讓你們起膿瘡！

普洛斯帕羅：為你說了這些話，我要懲罰你：今晚你會全身抽筋，腰如刀刺，痛得讓你喘不過氣來。小妖精會整晚狠狠捏你，比被蜜蜂叮還要疼，最後你的皮膚會變成一個蜂窩。

卡列班：我要吃我的晚餐。這座島是我的，是我媽媽席考拉克斯的，是你從我手中奪走的。你剛來的時候，撫摸我，對我好，給我有漿果味道的水喝。你教我如何稱呼白天燃燒的大光，如何稱呼晚上閃爍的小光。因為愛你，我帶你去看這個島上的所有一切──清泉、鹽井、荒地、肥田，我活該倒楣要告訴你這些！但願席考拉克斯的所有詛咒──蟾蜍、甲蟲、蝙蝠──全部都降在你身上！我是你唯一擁有的僕人──我曾是這座島的國王，現在卻被你關在這個硬石洞穴裡，與世隔絕。

普洛斯帕羅：你這個說謊的奴才！仁慈對你是沒有用的，要用酷刑。你雖然面目可憎，我卻以仁義待你，讓你睡在我的洞穴，但你卻試圖染指我的女兒！

卡列班：歐吼！歐吼！我真希望我得逞！如果不是你阻止了我的話，這座島上就有一堆小卡列班啦！

米蘭達：你這個骯髒的奴隸！良善對你起不了任何作用，你從頭到腳都是邪惡。我看你可憐，辛辛苦苦教你說人話，每一分時光都費盡心思教導你。那時候，你這野蠻人，還不懂得表達自己的思想，只會像個牲畜呼嚕呼嚕的叫。我教導你把想法表達成為話語，但是你這個骯髒的傢伙，即便學了人話，骨子裡卻還是禽獸。所以，把你關在這裡也只是適得其所，儘管你應受的懲罰比這個還要更多。

卡列班：你教我說話，唯一的用處就是我學到該如何詛咒。願瘟疫降臨在你身上，讓你長紅瘡，活該你教我說話！

普洛斯帕羅：滾開，你這個女巫的兒子！去給我撿些木材來，快點。（卡列班聳聳肩，滿臉不在乎樣。）你剛才聳肩了嗎？混帳傢伙？敢不聽我的話，或心不甘情不願，我就讓你全身抽筋，骨頭發疼，讓你哭喊到連野獸聽到都發寒。

卡列班（害怕得發抖）：不，求求你不要。（竊語：）我必須聽他的話，他的法術很厲害，甚至連我媽媽拜的神，瑟底堡斯，都得聽他的話。

普洛斯帕羅：還不趕快去，奴才！

（卡列班下。菲迪南上，後面跟著只有普洛斯帕羅看的見的愛麗兒。愛麗兒彈著魯特琴。）

愛麗兒（唱歌）：

跟我來這黃色的沙灘，

讓我們手牽著手，

行禮，親吻，讓海浪停止，

輕舞漫步著每一寸地方，

甜美的精靈為你合唱，

聽啊，仔細聽……

合唱：汪汪汪！看門狗吠叫！汪汪。

愛麗兒：聽啊，聽，我聽到雞啼，咕咕咕。

菲迪南：這音樂是從哪裡來的？天上，還是人間？（他仔細聽著。）音樂停了，當然啊，這是給這座島上的神仙聽的。當我在岸邊坐下，為死去的國王，也就是我的父親哭泣時，這首音樂的美妙旋律撫慰著我，也讓大海平靜。我跟隨著音樂，來到這裡，或是說它將我帶來這裡。但是音樂消失了。不！它又開始了。

愛麗兒：

你的父親埋在海底五噚深處，

他的屍骨已化為珊瑚，

他的眼睛成為了珍珠，

他的一切都化成腐朽，

經過全然的轉化，

蛻變成珍寶奇物，

海仙女敲著他的喪鐘。

合唱：叮咚。

愛麗兒：聽啊！我聽到了，叮咚的鐘聲。

菲迪南：這首歌在唱我那淹死的父親，這不是大自然的音樂，也並非是人世間的樂章，它從我的頭上傳來。

普洛斯帕羅（對米蘭達）：張開你的眼睛，告訴我你看到什麼。

米蘭達（欣賞著菲迪南）：那是什麼？精靈嗎？上天啊，他正在環顧四周。父親，相信我，他是這樣的好看，可惜他是精靈。

普洛斯帕羅：不，我的女兒。他和我們一樣會吃會睡，擁有人類的知覺。眼前的這位紳士剛經歷了船難，除去悲傷所帶來的疤痕外，他確實是位美男子。他和朋友走丟了，現在正在尋找他們。

米蘭達：我會稱他為神祇，因為我在世上從沒看過這麼高貴的人物。

普洛斯帕羅（竊語）：事情如我所願！（對愛麗兒：）精靈，我的好精靈，因為這件事我兩天之內就會讓你自由！

菲迪南（看著米蘭達）：這一定是音樂所吟唱的女神。（對米蘭達：）請允許我卑微地請教，您是否住在這座島上？請告訴我在這裡要如何自處，還有，啊，女神，我最想要請教您的問題是，您是否是人間的女子？

米蘭達：我一點也不美，先生，但我的確是人間的女子。

菲迪南：天啊！你會說我的語言？如果我現在在自己的國家的話，我一定是會說這種語言的人當中最尊貴的人了！

普洛斯帕羅：什麼，最尊貴？如果那不勒斯王聽到你這番話，不知道會作何感想？

菲迪南：如同現在的我，一個孤獨的人，我很訝異你提到了那不勒斯。他聽到了我說的話，正因如此，更讓我悲泣——因為我現在就是那不勒斯王。我親眼目睹我的父親，也就是那不勒斯王，遇到了船難而殞落，自此便悲痛不已。

米蘭達：唉，真是可憐！

菲迪南：是的，還有他的大臣們，米蘭公爵和他那勇敢的兒子，也遭遇了不測。

普洛斯帕羅（竊語）：真正的米蘭公爵和他那更勇敢的女兒可以證明你是錯的，如果現在時機成熟的話。（看著菲迪南和米蘭達）這真是一見鍾情，可愛的愛麗兒，為了這件事我一定會給你自由。（對菲迪南：）先生，我和你說一句話。我想你錯了，我和你說……

米蘭達：為什麼父親說話如此無理？他是我第三個看過的男人，也是第一個我為他嘆息的男人，希望我父親和我一樣同情他的遭遇！

菲迪南：啊，倘若你仍是黃花閨女，尚未將你的愛寄託給他人。倘若是這樣的話，我一定會讓你成為那不勒斯王后！

普洛斯帕羅：這樣就足夠了，先生，我和你說……（竊語：）他們兩人為彼此著迷，所以我得讓他們嚐些苦頭，容易得來的愛情不足以珍惜。（對菲迪南：）再和你說一句，你給我聽好，你這個騙子，你一定是來這裡當間諜的，想從我手上奪取這座島嶼，成為島主。

菲迪南：不是的，我以自己的名聲立誓！

米蘭達：奸邪是不會住在廟堂的！如果惡靈會住在如此俊美的廟堂的話，美德也會想住在裡面！

普洛斯帕羅（對菲迪南）：跟我過來。（對米蘭達：）不要為他說話。他是叛徒。（對菲迪南：）來，我要把你的脖子和腳都上銬，你只能喝海水，吃貽貝、枯根、玉米殼，跟我過來！

菲迪南：不！除非我的敵人比我強大，否則我是不會答應的。

（他拔出了他的劍，但是普洛斯帕羅對他施咒，讓他動彈不得。）

米蘭達：天啊，親愛的父親，別對他如此殘忍。他是位紳士，不會想加害你的。

普洛斯帕羅：什麼？你以為我腦袋不清嗎？（對菲迪南：）奸細，把劍放下。你只是做做樣子，但卻不敢攻擊。你的良知充滿了罪惡，我用這根手杖便可以讓你繳械，（他揮動手杖，將菲迪南的劍打落。）並讓你的劍掉落地上。

米蘭達：求求你，父親。

普洛斯帕羅：走開！不要拉我的衣服！

米蘭達：父親，可憐他吧！我為他擔保。

普洛斯帕羅：閉嘴！再說我就要責罵你了，你想幫騙子說話嗎？給我安靜！你這個笨女孩！你以為這世上沒有比他更好的人了嗎？和其他人比起來，他只是個卡列班，別人都是天使。

米蘭達：我的要求極其卑微，我不想遇見更英俊的男人。

普洛斯帕羅（對菲迪南）：來吧，服從我的命令。你的肌肉像嬰兒一樣，一點力氣也沒有。

菲迪南：的確，我漸漸失去了知覺，好像在作夢一樣，父親的死去、我的軟弱、船難遇害的朋友、還有這個人對我的威脅——這些都算不了什麼。我只要能夠每天見到這位小姐一回，關在牢裡也無所謂，讓別人享受其餘的世界吧，我在這牢裡的小角落就已心滿意足。

普洛斯帕羅（竊語）：成功了。（對菲迪南：）來吧。（對愛麗兒：）做得好，我的好愛麗兒，隨我來。我來告訴你你接下來要做的事。

米蘭達（對菲迪南）：不要擔心，我的父親比你所想的還要善良，

只是現在他有點反常。

普洛斯帕羅（對愛麗兒）：你將如山風一般自由，但要照我的話去做。

愛麗兒：每個字都會遵從。

普洛斯帕羅（對菲迪南）：來吧，隨我來。（對米蘭達：）不要幫他説話。

（全體下。）

第二幕

●第一場 ————————————P. 045

在島的另一邊，阿隆佐、瑟拜士梯安、安東尼奧、貢札羅、阿特利安、法朗西斯科還有其他的生還者上。

貢札羅：各位，求求你們，快樂一點吧，我們有著快樂的理由，我們的倖存比我們的損失來的有價值。每天，水手的妻子、船東、商人，都有和我們一樣的理由傷心難過，但是百萬人當中卻很少有人像我們一樣可以幸運地生還。所以，親愛的朋友們，我們要好好地想想，究竟是應該難過，還是慶幸。

阿隆佐：拜託，請你安靜！

瑟拜士梯安（對安東尼奧竊語）：他接受安慰的態度好像拿到一碗冷粥一樣。

安東尼奧（對瑟拜士梯安，嘲弄貢札羅）：這位大善人可沒那麼輕易放棄安慰人的。

瑟拜士梯安（對安東尼奧表示同意）：看好，他在轉動智慧的發條。（貢札羅仔細思索應該說什麼。）隨時他就會繼續敲鐘了。

貢札羅（對阿隆佐）：陛下，當一個人已經經歷過所有的不幸時，那他可就大大的——

瑟拜士梯安：大大的有賞，一塊錢嗎？

貢札羅：平靜會和他同在的，你說的比懂的還要多。

瑟拜士梯安：你比我想像的還要聰明得多。

貢札羅：所以，陛下——

安東尼奧：天啊，他可真說得沒完沒了啊！

阿隆佐（對貢札羅）：拜託，安靜下來。

貢札羅：我不說了，但是——

瑟拜士梯安：他還要繼續說啊！

安東尼奧（對瑟拜士梯安）：來打個賭，這兩個人——貢札羅還是阿特利安——誰會先開口？

瑟拜士梯安（輕聲回話）：我賭貢札羅！

安東尼奧：我賭阿特利安！

瑟拜士梯安：好！（兩人握手。）我們賭什麼？

安東尼奧：賭好玩就好。

瑟拜士梯安：一言為定！

阿特利安：雖然這座島看似荒蕪——

安東尼奧（大笑）：哈，哈，哈！

瑟拜士梯安（對安東尼奧）：好吧，你贏了！

阿特利安（繼續說）：路又難走——

瑟拜士梯安（小聲對安東尼奧）：他會說但是——

阿特利安：但是——

安東尼奧（小聲回瑟拜士梯安）：我就知道！

阿特利安（沒有發覺瑟拜士梯安和安東尼奧在嘲笑他）：天氣似乎
很溫和、甜美、柔弱。

安東尼奧（輕推了瑟拜士梯安一下）：我認識一個這樣的女孩！

瑟拜士梯安：一定是位美人兒，他說的真好。

阿特利安：輕風在這裡甜美地吹拂。

瑟拜士梯安（對安東尼奧）：好像風有壞掉的肺可以呼吸一樣。

安東尼奧（回瑟拜士梯安）：沼澤吹來的臭氣還差不多。

貢札羅：美好的事物都在我們眼前。

安東尼奧（竊語）：對，除了必需品之外什麼都有。

瑟拜士梯安（竊語）：不是只有一些，就是什麼都沒有！

貢札羅：綠茵草地看來多麼地茂盛而健康啊！

安東尼奧（竊語）：事實上只是一片乾涸的大地。

瑟拜士梯安（竊語）：以及一小片的綠地。

安東尼奧（竊語）：他也不算説錯。

瑟拜士梯安（竊語）：沒錯，不過也沒全對……

貢札羅：最奇特的是，這真是令人難以相信——

瑟拜士梯安（竊語）：令人難以相信的事都很奇特。

貢札羅：——我們的衣服，雖然浸在海裡，卻像新的一樣。

安東尼奧（竊語）：他接下來還會説什麼新奇的話呢？

瑟拜士梯安（竊語）：他會把這座島放入他的口袋，當成一顆
　　蘋果一樣送給他的兒子。

安東尼奧（竊語）：他會把蘋果核種在海裡，生出更多的島嶼。

貢札羅（對阿隆佐）：我的外套看起來是不是像新的一樣，就像
　　我第一次穿上它參加您女兒在突尼斯舉辦的婚禮？

阿隆佐：我真希望我沒有參加我女兒嫁給突尼斯王的婚禮，
　　這趟回程讓我失去了兒子！同時嫁了女兒，好像也失去了女
　　兒。她現在遠離了義大利，恐怕我再也見不到她了！啊，我
　　的兒子，那不勒斯及米蘭的繼承人，你成了哪隻怪魚的大
　　餐呢？

法朗西斯科：陛下，他或許還活著。我看到他奮力地掙扎，爬
　　上了波浪。他努力待在海面之上，勇敢地抬起頭面對迎來
　　的海浪，我相信他平安無事地上岸了。

阿隆佐：不，不，他死了，他死了！

瑟拜士梯安：陛下，您給自己帶來這一重大的損失，倒是應該
　　感謝您自己。您不讓您的女兒為我們歐洲人祈福，反倒是讓

她嫁給一個非洲人，因為這樣，或許您再也看不到她了，這就足夠讓您流淚了！

阿隆佐：拜託，請別再說了。

瑟拜士梯安：我們都請求您三思而行，您可憐的女兒，掙扎於拒絕或服從您的賜婚之間而無所適從。現在，恐怕您連兒子都失去了。因為您的決定，米蘭和那不勒斯的寡婦比可以安慰他們的男人要來得多，這全部的錯都要算在您身上！

阿隆佐：這的確是極大的損失。

貢札羅：瑟拜士梯安爵士，你說的雖然是實話，但有失禮數，時機也不對。在你該幫忙治病的時候，你卻揭開傷疤。

瑟拜士梯安：你說的對。

安東尼奧：應該像醫生一樣！

貢札羅：你的憂鬱給我們所有人帶來了壞天氣，好先生。

瑟拜士梯安：壞天氣？

安東尼奧：非常壞。

貢札羅（無視他們）：陛下，如果我住在這座島上的話──

安東尼奧（竊語）：他會到處種蕁麻。

瑟拜士梯安（竊語）：或是野草、草藥之類的。

貢札羅：在我的完美國家裡，我會讓我的國度變得完全不一樣。不會有法官，人民不需要讀書。富貴、貧窮、奴隸也不會出現在這個國度。沒有契約、沒有繼承權、沒有國界、沒有籬笆、沒有農耕、沒有葡萄園。不需要金屬、玉米、酒，或是油。我的人民不需要工作，每個男人每天都無所事事，女人也是。所有的人都善良純真。沒有國王——

瑟拜士梯安（竊語）：他不是說自己要當國王嗎！

安東尼奧（竊語）：最後一部分和前面講的不一樣。

貢札羅：大自然供應所有我們需要的東西，我們不需要揮汗辛勤地工作。不會有叛變、犯罪、劍矛刀槍和砲彈。大自然會提供所有的糧食，供應給我天真無邪的子民。我的國家治理地完美無瑕，更勝黃金盛世。

瑟拜士梯安：上帝保佑這位君王！

安東尼奧：願貢札羅陛下萬壽無疆！（他們嘲笑著他。）

貢札羅：另外——陛下，您有在聽我說嗎？

阿隆佐：我求求你，別再說了，你說的話毫無意義！

貢札羅：您說的一點也沒錯，陛下。我說這些話為的只是娛樂這些王公貴族，他們過於敏感好動，卻總是不知道為何發笑。

安東尼奧：我們笑的是你。

貢札羅：這種愚昧的訕笑，我比不上你們，所以你們繼續無意義地笑吧。

安東尼奧：這記回馬槍使得真是漂亮！

瑟拜士梯安（繼續嘲弄貢札羅）：只可惜用的是毫無殺傷力的部位！

貢札羅：你們字字機鋒，如果月亮連續五星期都不動的話，你們甚至可以用你們的話語將她搬離軌道！

（愛麗兒上，他隱形著，彈奏著莊嚴的音樂。）

安東尼奧（對貢札羅）：大人，別發脾氣。

貢札羅：當然不會，我不會為那麼小的事生氣。不如你們繼續嘲笑我，好讓我睡著？我很累了。

安東尼奧：睡吧，聽我們笑你。（他大笑。）

（每個人都睡了，除了阿隆佐、瑟拜士梯安、和安東尼奧。）

阿隆佐：什麼，大家這麼快就都睡了！真希望我可以閉起眼睛就將我的思緒閉鎖起來，他們是真的想關起來了。

瑟拜士梯安：陛下，那就睡吧，不用逞強。睡眠很少拜訪傷心的人，當它來臨時，它帶來的是慰藉。

安東尼奧：您睡著的時候，我們兩個會守護著您，我們會保護您。

阿隆佐：謝謝你們。（他打著哈欠，伸著懶腰。）我真的累得想睡了……

（他很快地睡著。愛麗兒下。）

瑟拜士梯安：睡意竟然如此奇怪地降臨在他們身上！

安東尼奧：是這裡空氣的原因吧。

瑟拜士梯安：那麼為什麼我們一點睡意都沒有？我一點也不累。

安東尼奧：我也是，清醒得很。他們都倒在一起，好像說好同時睡去一樣，又好像同時被雷電擊中一樣。(他停了一下，思忖著。)如果，瑟拜士梯安，唉呀，如果說──？(他停頓了一樣，不敢繼續往下說。)我最好不要往下說了。但是，我從你臉上可以看到你未來的樣子，在我的想像中，我看到一頂王冠落在你的頭上。

瑟拜士梯安：什麼？你是清醒的嗎？

安東尼奧：你沒有在聽我說話嗎？

瑟拜士梯安：聽到了，但是你好像在胡言亂語，你在說夢話嗎？你說什麼？這真是奇怪的睡法，睡覺的時候眼睛張開著，一邊說話一邊睡覺。

安東尼奧：高貴的瑟拜士梯安，你正在讓你的大好機會睡著──或是說死去！你醒著的時候竟把眼睛閉上。

瑟拜士梯安：你的鼾聲很清楚，鼾聲之中帶有意義。

安東尼奧：我比平常更認真地說話，如果你想聽我的忠告你也得這樣。要是你聽了我的建議，你的地位會比現在更偉大三倍以上。

瑟拜士梯安：好吧，我像是一灘靜止的水──還不確定會往哪個方向流去。

安東尼奧：讓我來教你往哪個方向流。

瑟拜士梯安：請繼續說，你的眼神和表情似乎告訴我你有很重要的事情要說，你好像已經準備要一吐為快了。

安東尼奧：是這樣的，大人。(他向著貢札羅點點頭。)這個健忘的老頭，當他死後下葬就該被遺忘，但他卻差一點就成功說服國王他的兒子沒有死。他不可能沒有淹死，除非他可以一邊睡覺一邊游泳。

瑟拜士梯安：我對他還活著不抱一點希望。

安東尼奧：啊，別說沒有希望的話了，你該想的是你的希望有多大呢？從這邊看是沒有希望，但另一方面來說的希望就很高了，高到野心平時都不敢奢望，你也同意菲迪南已經淹死了吧？

瑟拜士梯安：他死了。

安東尼奧：那誰將是那不勒斯的繼承人？

瑟拜士梯安：克拉莉貝兒。

安東尼奧：她現在是突尼斯王后，距離荒煙漫草都有三十里之遙。她不會得到來自那不勒斯的消息，月亮上的那個人走路太慢了，除非讓太陽當起信使。離開克拉莉貝兒之後，我們就遇到船難了。有些人漂流到這座島上，這是命中註定的，我們準備要演一齣戲。這齣戲的開場白已經過去了，剩下的部份得由你我來主演。

瑟拜士梯安：我聽不懂你說的話？這到底是什麼意思？我哥哥的女兒是突尼斯王后，但她同時也是那不勒斯的繼承人，這兩個地方距離很遙遠。

安東尼奧：而這段距離的每一吋都在叫喊著：「那個克拉莉貝兒怎麼可能回到那不勒斯呢？留在突尼斯吧，讓那個瑟拜士梯安醒來！」如果這些睡著的人都變成死人的話，其實和他們現在這樣也沒多大差別。有個人可以和現在睡著的這一位一樣統治那不勒斯，很多大臣可以像這個不足掛齒的貢札羅一樣嘮叨不休，我可以把一隻鸚鵡教到和他一樣愛說廢話。啊，如果你想的和我一樣！這場沉睡真是意義重大

—— (他指著貢札羅、阿隆佐、阿特利安、和法朗西斯科。) ——

對你的未來而言！你聽懂我的話嗎？

瑟拜士梯安：我想我懂。

安東尼奧：那你覺得如何？

瑟拜士梯安：我記得你當年推翻了你的哥哥普洛斯帕羅……

安東尼奧：是的，看看我現在身上的衣服多麼合身，比以前那件來的合身。我哥哥的下屬以前是我的同儕，現在都臣服於我。

瑟拜士梯安：你的良心不會過意不去嗎？

安東尼奧：好問題，大人，良心在哪裡呢？二十個良心站在我和米蘭中間，他們表面堅如冰石，但是我下定決心後，立刻就融化了。你的哥哥現在躺在這裡，跟泥土一樣一動也不動。（他拔出匕首。）這把聽話的劍，可以讓他永遠躺在那裡。我動手的時候，你可以讓這老頭（他指著貢札羅）永遠閉上眼。我們不會想要他來批評我們的行為，其他的人，他們會乖乖地聽著我們教他們的故事，就像是貓舔著牛奶一樣。我們說什麼，他們信什麼。

瑟拜士梯安：我的好友，你的例子激勵著我。你得到米蘭，我得到那不勒斯。拔劍吧，一劍砍下，將免去你所有的納貢，而我這個新任國王，將會成為你的好友。

安東尼奧：一起拔劍吧，我舉劍，你也舉劍。我的劍落下，你也讓貢札羅人頭落地。

瑟拜士梯安：我還有一句話要說……

（他把安東尼奧拉到一邊，同時愛麗兒上，他依然隱身著，走向貢札羅。）

愛麗兒：我的主人用法術預知了你的災難，他派我來救你們大家，否則的話，他的計畫就要失敗。（愛麗兒對著貢札羅耳朵唱歌。）

當你鼾聲作響時，

密謀正張著眼睛抓緊時機，

如果你珍惜自己的生命，

趕快除掉睡意，你得有所警惕，

醒來，醒來！

安東尼奧（回到原位，高舉起劍）：我們趕快行事！

貢札羅（突然醒來）：願天使保佑吾王！

（眾人也跟著醒來，臉露驚恐。）

阿隆佐（一臉狐疑的說）：發生了什麼事？（對安東尼奧說：）你拔劍做什麼？為什麼你的臉這麼可怕？

貢札羅：發生什麼事了？

瑟拜士梯安（把劍放下，急中生智）：我們守護您的時候，突然聽到了一聲怒吼。聽起來像是牛的聲音，又好像是獅子。這聲音沒有吵醒您嗎？我可是被嚇了一跳。

阿隆佐：我什麼都沒聽到，你聽到了嗎，貢札羅？

貢札羅：陛下，我聽到一陣嗡嗡聲（很奇怪的聲音），這聲音讓我醒來。我睜開眼睛的時候，就看到他們拔劍。是真的有一陣噪音，我們最好保持警戒，或是離開這裡，一起拔劍戒備吧。

阿隆佐：帶路，繼續尋找我那可憐的兒子。

貢札羅：但願上天保佑他遠離這些可怕的野獸——他一定在這座島上。

阿隆佐：帶路吧。

愛麗兒：普洛斯帕羅一定會知道我做的一切，國王，安心地去找你的兒子吧。

（全體下。）

●第二場 ———————————————— P. 062

在島嶼的另一端。卡列班上，他扛著一堆木材。遠方傳來雷電的聲音。

卡列班：願太陽從沼澤吸起的瘴癘之氣都降臨在普洛斯帕羅身上，讓他生病！（丑角屈林鳩羅上。）這個一定是他的精靈，因為我搬木材太慢來修理我的。我躺平在地上，躲在衣服裡，讓他看不到我。

屈林鳩羅：這裡沒有灌木樹叢可以讓我躲避，聽這風的聲音，看來暴風雨又在醞釀了。天上的黑雲好像一個大酒桶，隨時準備爆發，把酒噴出來。如果它像平常那樣打雷的話，我不知道要躲到哪裡，這朵雲看來會下起一桶一桶的雨。（他看到卡列班。）這是什麼？人還是魚？死的還是活的？應該是魚吧？聞起來像魚，他有一種古老的味道，他是一隻長相奇怪的魚！如果我在英格蘭的話，我會把這隻魚塗上顏色，一堆笨蛋就會為了看這隻怪魚而給我銀幣，但是他們卻一毛錢都不會給一個跛腳乞丐！（他更仔細看了卡列班。）等一下！

這不是魚！他看起來像是島上的人，被雷電打死了。(雷聲作響，比原先大聲。)啊，不！暴風雨又回來了，我要躲哪裡才好？不幸給人一個奇怪的床伴，看來我只好和這個死人一起躲雨了。(他爬到卡列班衣服裡面，頭腳相對。)

(斯蒂芬諾上，他唱著歌，手上還拿著酒瓶。)

斯蒂芬諾(唱歌)：

我再也不要出海，不要出海。

我就要死在這裡，在這岸邊。

這是首很爛的歌，葬禮唱的歌。

(喝一口酒)真好，這真是我的安慰。

(繼續唱歌)船長、船員、還有我都愛的茉莉、瑪格、瑪力安、瑪格麗，

但是沒人在乎凱特，

因為她舌頭有鈴鐺，

每次都會對水手大吼，「去死吧！」

她討厭焦油和瀝青的味道，

但是當裁縫給她搔癢時，她會咯咯地笑！

到海上吧，好男兒，讓她被吊死吧！

這真是一首爛歌。

(他將酒瓶拿靠在嘴邊。)但是這真是我的安慰！

卡列班(對屈林鳩羅說)：別折磨我！(他哀嚎。)啊！

斯蒂芬諾：這是什麼啊？有魔鬼嗎？(他檢查了一下地上，看到兩雙腿——分別是卡列班和屈林鳩羅的——凸了出來。)你想用野獸和怪胎來騙我嗎？我都逃過淹死的命運了，還會怕你們的四隻腳嗎？

卡列班（當屈林鳩羅移動時）：精靈在折磨我了，啊！

斯蒂芬諾：這隻島上怪物一定是發高燒了，他是怎麼會說人話的？讓我來醫治他吧。如果他有問題的話，我會讓他好起來，讓他聽話，帶他回那不勒斯，腳上穿鞋子的君王都會喜歡這個禮物的。

卡列班（對屈林鳩羅哀求）：求求你不要折磨我，我求你了，我下次搬木材會快一點。

斯蒂芬諾：他發顛了，胡言亂語。來給他嚐一口我酒瓶裡的好東西，如果他沒嘗過，這可以治療他的病症。如果我能治好他、讓他聽話的的話，我不會跟他收太多錢──但是該多少就多少！（靠近卡列班）來吧，把嘴打開，這個東西可以讓你不再顫抖。

屈林鳩羅：這個聲音！我聽過！他不是淹死了嗎？天啊，這是魔鬼啊！救命啊！

斯蒂芬諾：四隻腳加上兩個聲音，這是什麼怪物啊！前面的嘴巴說著好聽的話，後面的嘴巴罵聲連連。即使要喝光我的酒才能治好他的話，我也得這麼做，來吧。（他把酒倒進卡列班的喉嚨。）這樣就夠了。（換到屈林鳩羅。）好，我現在要倒進你的另一張嘴。

屈林鳩羅：斯蒂芬諾！

斯蒂芬諾：你另一張嘴在叫我嗎？天啊，這是魔鬼啊，不是怪物！

屈林鳩羅：斯蒂芬諾，如果你真的是斯蒂芬諾，碰我一下，和我說話。我是屈林鳩羅，別害怕，我真的是你的朋友，屈林鳩羅。

斯蒂芬諾：如果你真的是屈林鳩羅，就上前來。（他抓住屈林鳩羅的腳。）我抓住你兩隻腳，如果是屬於屈林鳩羅的話，應該就是他們了。（屈林鳩羅伸直了雙腳。）真的，你真的是屈林鳩羅！你怎麼會和這傢伙混在一起？

屈林鳩羅：我以為他被雷劈死了，可是你不是淹死了嗎，斯蒂芬諾？暴風雨結束了沒有？我因為怕暴風雨，所以躲在這怪物的衣服裡面。所以你沒死嗎，斯蒂芬諾？

（他將斯蒂芬諾轉來轉去，仔細端詳。）

斯蒂芬諾：拜託別把我轉來轉去好嗎！我胃很不舒服！

卡列班（竊語）：這些人倘若不是精靈，那他們一定是好人。他一定是勇敢的天神，帶著天上的水，我要向他跪拜。

斯蒂芬諾：你是怎麼來這裡的？你要以這瓶酒發誓！我是抱著一個水手丟下來的酒桶逃生的，這個瓶子是我被沖上岸後用手扒樹皮做的。

卡列班（跪在斯蒂芬諾腳下）：我要以這個瓶子發誓，成為您的僕人，這水是天上才有的啊！

斯蒂芬諾（將酒瓶當作聖經交給屈林鳩羅）：告訴我，你是怎麼逃離船難的。

屈林鳩羅：我像一隻鴨子一樣遊上岸。

斯蒂芬諾（將酒瓶遞給屈林鳩羅）：給你，親吻一下聖經吧。（屈林鳩羅喝了一口。）

屈林鳩羅：你還有酒嗎？

斯蒂芬諾：我把酒藏在岸邊的洞穴裡。（看到卡列班跪在他腳下）好的，怪物！你的病現在如何了？

卡列班：您是從天上掉下來的嗎？

斯蒂芬諾：告訴你，我是從月亮來的，我就是月亮上的使者。

卡列班：我有看過您，而且我很崇拜您。

斯蒂芬諾（將酒遞給卡列班）：過來，對這個發誓，親一下聖
經。（卡列班喝了一些酒。）我等下再將酒加滿。

屈林鳩羅：託光線所賜，我才看清楚這隻怪物蠢得很，我怎麼
會怕他呢？真是隻沒用的怪物！（他嘲笑著。）月亮上的使者？
我沒看過這麼呆的怪物！（卡列班終於放下了酒。）喝的好，怪
物，痛快！

卡列班：我會帶您去看這個島上豐饒的地方，我會親吻您的
腳。求求你，當我的神！

（趁斯蒂芬諾有些睡意，他又來要酒喝。）

屈林鳩羅：真是隻邪惡的怪物。他的神睡覺時，他就搶酒來
喝。

卡列班：讓我親吻您的腳，我發誓會當您的僕人。

斯蒂芬諾：來吧，跪下發誓！（卡列班跪在腳跟前親吻。）

屈林鳩羅：看到這隻腦袋空空的怪物，我真的會笑死。

斯蒂芬諾：來吧，親吻我的手！

屈林鳩羅：這隻怪物醉了！真是噁心！

卡列班：我會帶您去看最好的泉水，我會撿拾最好的漿果給
您，我會幫您捕魚，找最好的木材讓您保暖，我不會再幫我
服侍的那個暴君搬木材了，願瘟疫降臨在那個我服侍的暴
君身上。天神啊，我現在開始追隨您了。

屈林鳩羅：最可笑的怪物，竟然崇拜一個酒鬼！

卡列班：求求您，讓我帶您去蘋果生長的地方，我的長指甲可以幫您挖落花生，我會帶您去看松鴉的鳥巢，教您如何設陷阱捕捉小猴子，我會獻給您一大堆松果，還會幫您從岩石上抓海鷗的雛鳥，請跟我來吧。

斯蒂芬諾：帶路吧，別多話。屈林鳩羅，國王和其他人都淹死了，這座島就歸我們兩個管理了。

卡列班（酒醉唱歌）：再會了，我的主人！

屈林鳩羅（用手搗著耳朵）：鬼吼鬼叫的怪物！酒醉的怪物！

卡列班（唱歌）：

我不再捕魚，

不再為他砍柴，

我不再修補碗或洗碗。

班，班，卡列班，

現在有新主人了！新主人！

自由，高興的一天，快樂的一天！

自由，自由，高興的一天！

斯蒂芬諾：啊，勇敢的怪物！帶路！

（全體下。）

第三幕

●第一場 ——————————————— P. 073

在普洛斯帕羅的洞穴前，菲迪南上，扛著一塊木材。

菲迪南： 有些工作是勞苦的，但是這些痛苦卻有著歡欣的獎勵。有些屈辱是在尊嚴底下進行的，最卑微的工作有最值得獲取的目的。我現在做的工作既繁重又無趣，但我是為我心愛的人而做。她為死寂帶來新生，讓我從苦工中獲得無窮的快樂。啊！她比她的父親溫柔十倍，他父親根本是嚴厲的化身。我一天得搬上幾千塊這樣的木材，將它們堆好，否則就要接受懲罰。我那甜美的姑娘看到我辛苦地工作，總要流淚，她說這種粗重的工作不該由我來做。我一定是在做白日夢，但是這甜美的想法讓我的工作變的輕鬆，一想到我那美麗的姑娘，我就更努力工作。

（米蘭達上，普洛斯帕羅跟隨在後，他隱身著。）

米蘭達： 唉，我求你別再那麼賣力工作了！我真希望天上一把火將這些你要堆的木材都燒光。求求你，把手上的木材放下，休息一會兒吧。我父親正在書房看書，求求你休息一下吧！他接下來的三個小時都會忙著看書。

菲迪南： 啊，親愛的姑娘，我得在太陽下山之前把我的工作做完。

米蘭達： 如果你坐下來休息，我可以幫你搬一些木頭。求求你，讓我幫忙，我會搬到木堆那邊。

菲迪南： 不，珍貴的姑娘，我寧願拉斷我的筋骨，扭斷我的背，也不願讓你做這麼粗重的工作，而我卻在一旁休息。

米蘭達： 這工作可以讓你做，也可以讓我做。而且我做起來會

163

更容易，因為我的心是甘願的，而你是被迫的。

普洛斯帕羅（偷聽著）：我可憐的女兒，你已經陷入情網了，你所説的話證明了一切。

米蘭達：你看起來很累。

菲迪南：不，高貴的姑娘。當你在我身畔，夜晚都變成了清新的早晨。我請你告訴我——這樣我才知道禱告時要如何稱呼你——你叫什麼名字？

米蘭達：米蘭達。

菲迪南：令人傾心的米蘭達！世上最令人傾心的女子！這世上最美麗高貴的女子！我對許多女子動過情，許多次她們的甜言蜜語都叫我墜入愛河，但是她們當中沒有一個如此完美無瑕，總是有一點瑕疵讓她們的優美受損。但是你——你是如此完美，舉世無雙！你集世上美好於一身。

米蘭達：我沒有看過其他的女人，只有照鏡子的時候看過我自己的臉。除了你和我那親愛的父親之外，我也從未看過其他的男人。我一點都不知道其他人長的什麼樣子，但是這世上除了你之外，我也不想再認識其他人。

菲迪南：米蘭達，在地位上，我是一國的王子，或許也已經是國王了！我不會讓一隻蒼蠅飛進我的嘴巴，就如同我不可能像奴隸一樣搬這些木材。但是，請傾聽我的肺腑之言：我第一次看到你的時候，我的心就屬於你了。它停駐在你身上，情願當你的奴隸。因為你，我情願當個搬木工人。

米蘭達：你愛我嗎？

菲迪南：天地為證，若我説的是真話，願我的願望成真。如果我的言語有一絲空洞，願我一生所有的好運都變成不幸！我愛你、珍惜你、敬重你，超過世間所有的一切，無止無盡。

米蘭達（哭喊）：我真傻，竟為了聽到這樣的好消息而哭泣！

普洛斯帕羅（竊語）：真是兩個心靈契合的愛人啊！願上蒼保佑他倆！

菲迪南：你為什麼流淚呢？

米蘭達：因為我不值得，我不敢給你我想給的，也不敢從你那兒拿我想要的。我真蠢，我愈想掩飾隱藏，就讓一切愈加清楚明白！我不要令人臉紅的猜謎了！如果你願意娶我，我將成為你的妻子，如果你不想娶我，我寧願終生不嫁直到死去。

菲迪南：我的妻子，親愛的！我永遠是你的！

米蘭達：那你是我的丈夫嗎？

菲迪南：是的，我求之不得，如同奴隸渴望自由一般。握住我的手吧。

米蘭達：這是我的手，連同我的心一起交給你。再會了，半個鐘頭後再見。

菲迪南：一千個、一千個再會！

（米蘭達和菲迪南下，各自離開。）

普洛斯帕羅：真是令我高興啊！世上沒有比這件事更令我高興的。但是我得回到我的書房，研究法術。晚餐之前，我還有許多事情要做。

（普洛斯帕羅下。）

在島嶼的另一隅，卡列班、斯蒂芬諾和屈林鳩羅上。

斯蒂芬諾：好啦！酒喝完的時候，我們就喝水，但是要等到酒一滴不剩的那個時候。乾杯！（他喝了一口。）怪物僕人，你敬我一杯！

屈林鳩羅：怪物僕人！島上怪胎！他們說島上只有五個人，我們就佔了三個。如果另外兩個也和我們一樣瘋瘋癲癲的話，這個國家就完了！

斯蒂芬諾：我的半人半獸把他的舌頭泡在酒裡面了。至於我呢，大海可是淹不死我的！我可是游過三十五個聯邦，游來游去才到這座島上的。（對卡列班：）你可以當我的副官，或是掌旗手。

屈林鳩羅：當副官好了，我看他根本站不起來！

斯蒂芬諾：怪物，你自己認為呢？

卡列班：我的主人，您好嗎？讓我舔舔您的鞋子。（向屈林鳩羅點頭）我不會服侍他，他並非勇猛之人。

屈林鳩羅：你說謊，你這個無知的怪物。我勇敢到敢和警察對抗，你這隻邪惡的魚！你看過哪個懦夫可以喝下那麼多的酒嗎？你竟敢說這種駭人聽聞的謊話？

卡列班（對斯蒂芬諾）：您聽聽看他是如何嘲笑我的！我的大人，您可以忍受他這樣嗎？

屈林鳩羅：他說「大人」！天啊，沒看過這麼呆的怪物！

卡列班：您聽，您聽，他又說了，我求求您把他咬死！

斯蒂芬諾：屈林鳩羅，管好你那張嘴巴！這個可憐的怪物現在是我的屬下，你不可以污辱他。

卡列班：謝謝我高貴的主人，您願意再聽一次我的請求嗎？

斯蒂芬諾：當然，我會聽的。跪下，再說一次。

（愛麗兒上，隱身著。）

卡列班：如我之前所說，我為一個暴君工作，他是一個魔法師，他用奸計從我手上奪走了這座島。

愛麗兒：你說謊！

卡列班（以為是屈林鳩羅說的）：你才說謊，你這隻醜猴子！

斯蒂芬諾：屈林鳩羅，如果你繼續打斷他說的話，我會打地你滿地找牙。

屈林鳩羅：為什麼？我沒說話啊。

斯蒂芬諾：安靜！不要再說了！（對卡列班：）繼續說。

卡列班：我說，他用法術得到了這座島，他從我手上奪走了這座島。如果偉大的您可以幫我報仇的話，您可以當這座島的主人，我也會服侍您。

斯蒂芬諾：我要怎麼做？你會帶我去找他嗎？

卡列班：會的，我的大人。我會在他睡覺的時候帶您去找他，然後，您可以拿釘子敲進他的腦袋。

愛麗兒：你說謊，你辦不到的。

卡列班（以為屈林鳩羅又開口了）：怎麼會有這樣的蠢蛋呢！你這個白癡！（對斯蒂芬諾：）我懇求您，打他，把他的瓶子搶過來，讓他只能去喝鹽水，因為我不會告訴他清澈的泉水在哪裡。

斯蒂芬諾：屈林鳩羅，你給我注意了！再打斷我的怪物說話，我保證我不會對你客氣，我會把你打成肉餅！

屈林鳩羅：為什麼？我做了什麼？我什麼都沒做，我離你們遠一點好了。

愛麗兒：你説謊……

斯蒂芬諾：我説謊嗎？吃我一拳！（打屈林鳩羅）你喜歡被我打的話，再講我説謊看看。

屈林鳩羅：我沒有説你説謊啊，你是不是腦袋和耳朵都有問題？願天花長在你酒瓶上！這正是酒精和酗酒會帶給你的。願瘟疫降臨在你的怪物身上，讓魔鬼奪去你的手指！

卡列班：哈，哈，哈！

斯蒂芬諾（對卡列班説）：現在，繼續説你的故事吧。（對屈林鳩羅説：）你最好站遠一點。

卡列班：痛扁他，過一段時間，我也要扁他。

斯蒂芬諾（對屈林鳩羅，手指方向）：再遠一點！（對卡列班：）來，繼續説吧。

卡列班：好，他每到下午都要午睡，您可以趁那個時候打破他的腦袋，用木頭敲碎他的頭骨，或是割斷他的喉嚨。記得要先把他的書搶過來，他一旦沒有書，就跟我一樣沒有用，也不能召喚精靈，精靈都和我一樣討厭他，所以一定要把他的書燒掉。但是最有價值的東西是他那美麗的女兒，他自己説過她美如天仙，舉世無雙。我只看過兩個女人，我媽媽席考拉克斯和她，但是他女兒比席考拉克斯更貌美，就像天與地的差別一樣。

斯蒂芬諾：她真的有那麼美麗嗎？

卡列班：是的，大人，她一定會把您服侍的好好的，我保證，她會幫您生一堆小孩。

斯蒂芬諾：怪物，我一定要殺了這個人，他的女兒和我會成為王后和國王，上帝恩典啊！我讓屈林鳩羅和你成為總督。你還滿意這樣的劇本嗎，屈林鳩羅？

屈林鳩羅：好極了！

斯蒂芬諾：我們握手言和，很抱歉打了你，但注意一下你的言行。

卡列班：半個鐘頭後，他就會睡覺，您要那個時候去殺了他嗎？

斯蒂芬諾：是的，以我的名聲發誓。

愛麗兒（竊語）：我要將這件事告訴我的主人。

卡列班：我真高興，要不要唱那首您剛教我唱的歌？

斯蒂芬諾：為了你，怪物，我會為你做任何事。來吧，屈林鳩羅，一起歡唱吧。

（唱歌）

嘲笑他們，痛扁他們，

痛扁他們，嘲笑他們，

怎麼想都無所謂——

（愛麗兒打鼓吹笛伴奏。唱歌的人們嚇一跳，停了下來。）

斯蒂芬諾：什麼聲音？

屈林鳩羅（驚嚇）：我們的歌，有隱形人伴奏！

斯蒂芬諾：如果你是人的話，現形來。如果你是魔鬼的話，現出你想要的樣子給我們看！

屈林鳩羅（跪下）：啊，原諒我的罪過！

斯蒂芬諾（胸前畫十字）：悲憫我們！

卡列班：你們怕了嗎？

斯蒂芬諾（顫抖著）：不，怪物，我沒有。

卡列班：不用怕。這座島上充滿了怪聲，這些聲音帶來快樂，不會害人。

斯蒂芬諾：這王國真的適合我啊，我每天都有免費的音樂可以享受！

卡列班：當您解決了普洛斯帕羅之後……

斯蒂芬諾：很快。

屈林鳩羅：聲音不見了，跟著音樂，再來做我們的工作。

斯蒂芬諾：帶路，怪物，我們跟著你走。我真希望可以看到這個鼓手，打的真是不錯。

屈林鳩羅：我跟你後面，斯蒂芬諾。

（全體下。）

●第三場 ————————————————— P. 086

在島的另一隅，阿隆佐、瑟拜士梯安、安東尼奧、貢札羅、阿特利安、法朗西斯科還有其他人上。

貢札羅：陛下，我走不動了，我真的走不動了。如果您允許的話，我得休息一下！

阿隆佐：老人家，我不怪你。我自己也筋疲力盡了，坐下來休息一下吧。我放棄找我兒子了，唉，他淹死了，大海在嘲笑我們注定徒勞無功。算了，讓他去吧。

安東尼奧（對瑟拜士梯安竊語）：我很高興他終於放棄了希望，別忘了我們的計畫。

瑟拜士梯安（對安東尼奧）：我們要好好把握住下次的機會。

安東尼奧（對瑟拜士梯安）：就是今天晚上，他們會因為旅途勞累，不像白天一樣那麼有警覺性。

瑟拜士梯安（對安東尼奧）：好，就是今晚。

（莊嚴的音樂響起。普洛斯帕羅上，他隱身著。眾精靈搬上一桌酒席，圍著桌子跳舞，邀請國王和他的大臣一起享用，然後離開。）

阿隆佐：這是什麼音樂？朋友們，聽！

貢札羅：神奇美妙的音樂！

阿隆佐：那些人是誰？

瑟拜士梯安：活生生的布偶戲！不可思議！

貢札羅：如果我回到那不勒斯告訴大家的話，他們會相信我嗎？

阿隆佐：令人驚訝的是，這些長相奇特的精靈不需言語就可以溝通。

普洛斯帕羅（竊語）：等等再讚美吧。

法朗西斯科：他們突然消失了！

瑟拜士梯安：沒關係，他們把這酒席留下來了——而我們都非常餓了。（對國王：）你要享用嗎？

阿隆佐：我不要！

貢札羅：我覺得應該不會有事。

阿隆佐：好吧，我吃。如果這是我的最後一餐，也沒關係，反正我人生最好的時光已經過去了。

（雷電交加。愛麗兒上，化身為哈耳庇厄，神話中的鳥身女妖。他在酒席上拍動翅膀，食物隨之消失。）

愛麗兒：你們三個帶罪之身，是命運讓那永遠飢餓的大海把你們打嗝出來，使你們來到這座孤島上，你們是最不配活在人間的。（阿隆佐和其他人拔劍。）你們這群傻子！我和我的伙伴都是大自然的一部份，就和你們手上的劍的原料一樣！你們可以盡情對呼嘯的風砍擊、或者刺向大海，結果只會是你們仍舊動不到我一根羽毛！我的精靈伙伴和我一樣強壯，想傷害他們也是徒勞無功。你們聽好了——這是我來找你們的目的——你們三個人將心地善良的普洛斯帕羅從米蘭驅逐出境，把他和他的無辜的孩子放逐至海上。因為你們的惡行，神明興起了大海大浪，以及讓所有的生物來懲罰你們。祂們從你手中帶走了你的兒子，阿隆佐，透過我祂們要讓你一輩子徘徊受苦（比痛快死去更為痛苦），你將這樣度過你的餘生。如果你不想再觸怒神明的話，從今往後你得痛改前非，真心向善。

（愛麗兒在雷聲之中消失。然後，一陣柔和的音樂襲來，眾精靈一面帶走了酒席，一面以舞蹈嘲弄阿隆佐等人。）

普洛斯帕羅：我親愛的愛麗兒，你將哈耳庇厄演的真好。我要求的你都做到了，我的精靈們也做得很好，我的咒語都顯靈了，我的仇敵現在完全在我的控制之下，不知所措。就暫時讓他們這樣吧，我要去見見那個他們以為已經淹死的菲迪南，還有他的、也是我的，可愛女孩。

（普洛斯帕羅下。）

貢札羅（對阿隆佐）：陛下，您在看哪裡？

阿隆佐：真是可怕極了！海浪和風竟然對我說話，闡述我的罪過。我聽到雷聲說出了普洛斯帕羅這個名字，因為我的罪，我的兒子現在葬身於海底的淤泥中。我要去那裡找他，和他一起沉睡於泥濘之中。

（阿隆佐下，相當悲傷。）

瑟拜士梯安（挑釁）：一次對付一隻妖怪的話，我可以把他們全部擊垮！

安東尼奧：我來幫你。

（瑟拜士梯安和安東尼奧下。）

貢札羅：這三個人都瘋了。他們的罪行，好似慢性的毒藥，開始漸漸侵蝕他們的靈魂。我請求那些走路比較快的人趕快跟著他們後頭，阻止他們做出瘋狂的事。

阿特利安（對其他人）：跟在他們後面，快點！

（全體下，他們奔跑。）

第四幕

●第一場 P. 093

在普洛斯帕羅洞穴前，普洛斯帕羅、菲迪南和米蘭達上。

普洛斯帕羅：如果我對你太過嚴峻，你所獲得的獎勵或可彌補。我已將我的第三生命交託給你，她是我存活下來的目的。再一次，我讓你握著她的手。你的勞苦和試煉都是我測試你的愛的方式，而現在你通過考驗。啊，菲迪南，不要因為我誇耀她而笑我。你會清楚知道她超越所有的讚美之詞，所有的讚美都不及她的真實。

菲迪南：我知道你所說的都是事實。

普洛斯帕羅：好，這是我給你的禮物，也是你辛苦獲得的。我的女兒，就交給你了。但是記住，如果你在婚禮舉行之前和她共眠，你們的結合非但不會為上天所祝福，還會讓仇恨和衝突滋長。聽從我的話吧，直到大喜之日的那一天。

菲迪南：我要的是安靜的生活、平穩的家庭以及永久長存的愛情，我絕不會讓肉體的慾望消融我的榮譽。如果我犯了忌諱，這將作賤婚禮的喜悅，而時間將會永遠暫停，長夜將不會有盡頭。

普洛斯帕羅：說的好，坐下來和她說說話吧，她是你的人了。（呼叫）來，愛麗兒！

（愛麗兒上。）

愛麗兒：我偉大的主人有何吩咐？

普洛斯帕羅：你和你的助手們剛剛做得很好，我要你做另一件事。去找你的助手們來，我要讓這對新人看看我的法術，我向他們承諾過了，他們也滿心期盼著。

愛麗兒：現在嗎？

普洛斯帕羅：是的，一眨眼的時間。

愛麗兒：在你呼吸兩次的時間內，他們就會到了。你愛我嗎，
主人？

普洛斯帕羅：我非常愛你，我聰明伶俐的愛麗兒，我叫你的時
候你再出來。

愛麗兒：沒問題。

（愛麗兒下。）

第四幕
第一場

普洛斯帕羅（對菲迪南）：現在，你要遵守承諾，控制慾望，否則
你將和誓言道別。

菲迪南：我向你保證，先生，我愛人的潔白無暇冷卻了我炙熱
的慾望。

普洛斯帕羅：很好。來吧，愛麗兒。把你的助手帶上來，有多少
就帶多少，多多益善！來吧！快點！不要說話了！睜大你們的
雙眼！安靜！

（輕柔的音樂響起，精靈們開始表演。第一位出現的精靈扮作伊麗斯，
祂是彩虹女神亦是諸神信差。伊麗斯和刻瑞斯說話，刻瑞斯是農作
女神。）

伊麗斯：刻瑞斯，最慷慨的女神，你讓我們種植的小麥、黑麥、
大麥、和燕麥得以生長。你那滿山青翠的山林餵飽饑腸轆
轆的羊群，你那肥沃滋潤的草地讓他們的食物不虞匱乏。
你讓那花朵滿佈的河岸，在四月雨後水流不息。我是天空
之后所使那道彩虹的信差，請求你暫離尊榮的崗位，來到

此地，加入我們一同遊戲，不要遲疑！快點來吧，讓我們一起慶祝！

（刻瑞斯上，由愛麗兒扮演。）

刻瑞斯：伊麗斯，向你請安，多色的信使，天后朱諾的得意助手！告訴我，你的天后喚我來此細草綠地有何要事？

伊麗斯：慶祝真愛的締結，給予新人最大的祝福。

刻瑞斯：告訴我，上天的彩虹啊，維納斯和他兒子的丘比特仍然服侍著天后嗎？自從她們幫助冥王普魯托將我的女兒帶走之後，我已立誓不再與她們為伍。

伊麗斯：不用擔心她們，我在雲端看見她和她的兒子，她們對新人施咒，意圖讓新人背棄守身的誓言，但最後徒勞無功。火爆的維納斯已經回家，而她那寵壞的兒子丘比特也已將弓箭折斷，不再亂點鴛鴦譜，像個孩子般，成日與麻雀嬉戲。

刻瑞斯：偉大的天后朱諾來了，我認得她的步履。

（朱諾上。）

朱諾：我豐饒的姊妹們近來如何？和我一起來為這一對新人祝福，讓他們子孫滿堂，成就非凡。

（唱歌）

祝福你們尊榮與富貴，

祝福你們長壽與財富，

無時無刻的喜悅快樂，

朱諾在此歡唱祝福你們。

刻瑞斯（唱歌）：

五穀豐收，倉穀滿盈，

藤蔓結滿豐盈的果實，

植物長滿沉沉的作物，

豐收漫長，直到春天，

沒有匱乏和不足，

刻瑞斯為你們祝福。

菲迪南：這是我看過最莊嚴的景象，如此動人又如此和諧，他
們是精靈扮演的嗎？

普洛斯帕羅（點頭）：這些都是精靈，我的法術所召喚出來服從
我的吩咐的。

菲迪南：讓我永遠住在這裡好了，我的岳父如此睿智傑出，將
這個地方變成天堂。

（朱諾和刻瑞斯交頭接耳，讓伊麗斯離開準備另一項表演。）

普洛斯帕羅：噓，安靜！朱諾和刻瑞斯在細語，還有別的表演
要讓我們欣賞。

伊麗斯：水泉女神，帶著你那蘆葦花冠和和悅的臉孔，離開
你那點點漣漪的小溪，聽從天后的指示來到這片綠地。來
吧，溫柔的寧芙們，來此見證祝福真愛吧！別遲疑。（數位寧
芙上。）八月辛勤收割的農人，帶著你們被太陽曬黑的臉龐，
來到這片草地，快樂地休息。戴上你們的草帽，與寧芙共
舞。

（收割的農人穿戴整齊，上台，和優雅多姿的寧芙一起跳舞。快要結束
時，普洛斯帕羅突然開口，舞者遺憾地消失，只聞一陣奇異、空幽、
雜亂的聲音。）

普洛斯帕羅（竊語）：我差點忘了！卡列班那畜生和他黨羽的奸計。他們想加害於我，已經快到這裡了。（對眾精靈：）做的好！去吧！去吧！

菲迪南（對米蘭達）：真是奇怪，你父親激動不已。

米蘭達：我從來沒看他這麼生氣過。

普洛斯帕羅（看到菲迪南鬱鬱寡歡）：我的孩子，你看來憂慮不安。快樂點，我們的節目已經結束了。正如我跟你所說的，我們的演員都是精靈，在縹緲的空氣中消失，就像你所看見的景象都是虛幻的假象，高樓、宮廷、廟堂、土地本身、還有住在裡面的人，終將消逝。隨著表演煙消雲散，就連雲朵也不會留下一點痕跡。我們都是夢裡的幻影，我們的渺小生命都將在睡眠中循環輪迴。王子，我很生氣，所以請擔待我的弱點，我年邁的腦袋正在煩惱著。不要讓我的脆弱困擾你，如果你願意的話，請到我的洞穴稍做休息，我將散步片刻讓我的心靈歸於平靜。

菲迪南和米蘭達：願你的心得以平靜。

（菲迪南和米蘭達下。）

普洛斯帕羅：我用思想召喚你，謝謝你，愛麗兒！出現吧！

（愛麗兒上。）

愛麗兒：我和你心靈相通。你要我做什麼？

普洛斯帕羅：我們要準備去見卡列班。

愛麗兒：是的，我的主人。剛才在扮演刻瑞斯的時候，我本來要告訴你的，但是我深怕觸怒你。

普洛斯帕羅：再告訴我一次，這群混帳現在人在哪裡？

愛麗兒：他們喝得醉醺醺的，滿臉通紅，所以滿身勇氣。他們不斷揮打空氣，只因為空氣吹到他們臉上；痛擊地面，只因大地親吻他們腳下！然而他們正往這裡走來。我敲了鼓，他們就像是一群無堅不摧的小馬，豎起耳朵、睜大眼睛、挺起鼻子，仔細地聞著音樂。所以我對他們的耳朵下了咒，讓他們像一群小牛跟著我走過尖銳的荊棘樹叢，樹叢刺傷了他們的皮膚。最後我將他們留在靠近你住的洞穴的一處污泥水池，他們現在在那兒，手舞足蹈，把水池弄得比自己的腳還要臭。

普洛斯帕羅：做的好，愛麗兒！再隱身一會兒，去我的屋裡把一些微不足道的東西拿過來當誘餌，我們去抓這些賊。

愛麗兒：我這就去、我這就去。

（愛麗兒下。）

普洛斯帕羅（談論卡列班）：惡魔，真是天生的惡魔，本性不改。枉費我辛苦努力幫他改變劣根，一切枉然，白費力氣。隨著年紀，他身體愈來愈醜陋，心也愈變愈醜惡。（愛麗兒上，帶著閃閃發光的衣服和其他物件。）來吧，把這些東西掛在這裡。

（兩人隱身，將東西放好後退到後面。卡列班、斯蒂芬諾和屈林鳩羅上，渾身濕淋淋的。）

卡列班：拜託你們，放輕步伐，讓盲眼的鼬鼠都聽不到我們的聲音，我們已經快到他的洞穴了。

斯蒂芬諾：怪物，你還說那個精靈是沒有害處的，他做的可不只是耍些小把戲來愚弄我們而已。

卡列班：我的大人，請對我有點耐心。我為您帶來的禮物會讓您忘卻這場厄運。說話小聲點，現在和半夜一樣安靜。

屈林鳩羅：但是我們讓酒瓶掉進水池裡——

斯蒂芬諾：怪物，這不但是恥辱、羞辱，還是極大的損失！

屈林鳩羅：這比全身弄濕還糟，怪物，這就是你所說「沒有害處」的精靈！

斯蒂芬諾：我要去把我的酒瓶拿回來，就算淹死都沒關係！

卡列班：求求您，我的國王，請您安靜一下。看這裡，這就是洞穴的入口。進去的時候要安靜一點。這件大好的惡事做好的話，這座島就永遠是您的了。而我——您的卡列班——會永遠舔您的腳。

斯蒂芬諾：讓我握你的手，我開始有邪惡的念頭了。

屈林鳩羅（注意到掛著的漂亮衣服）：噢，天啊！噢，偉大的斯蒂芬諾！看看這個為你擺設的衣櫃。

卡列班：你這個笨蛋，別管這個，這只是些沒有用的東西。

屈林鳩羅（試穿一件長袍）：噢，不，怪物！我看得出什麼才是便宜貨！（四處炫耀）噢，斯蒂芬諾國王！

斯蒂芬諾：把衣服脫下來，屈林鳩羅。這件我要了！

屈林鳩羅（敬禮）：我的國王應當擁有它。（將衣服交給他。）

卡列班：願笨蛋都死去！你們為什麼要癡癡地看著這些衣服？別管衣服了，趕快動手殺人。如果他醒來的話，他會從頭到腳捏我們，折磨我們。他甚至還會將我們變成野鵝，或是額頭低窄的猩猩！

斯蒂芬諾：怪物，幫我們搬這些衣服，不然我把你趕出我的王國。這裡，拿好！（他們將衣服堆在卡列班身上。）

屈林鳩羅：還有這個。

斯蒂芬諾：對對，還有這個。

（打獵的聲音傳來。眾精靈上，化身為獵犬。牠們受普洛斯帕羅和愛麗兒差遣，去追擊斯蒂芬諾、屈林鳩羅和卡列班。）

普洛斯帕羅：嘿，魔山，攻擊！

愛麗兒：銀狼！去追，快！

普洛斯帕羅：怒火、怒火！在那裡，暴君，那裡！

（斯蒂芬諾、屈林鳩羅和卡列班被趕走。）

普洛斯帕羅（在狗群後吆喝）：去吧，告訴我的精靈們咬碎他們的關節，讓他們全身痙攣，用力捏他們身上的肉，讓他們身上的班點比豹來的多。

愛麗兒：聽他們狂吼的聲音！

普洛斯帕羅：讓他們盡情狩獵吧。現在，我所有的敵人都在我的掌控之下。我的工作即將完成，而你將如同空氣一般自由。聽我的命令行事並服從我吧，只要再一會兒。

（普洛斯帕羅和愛麗兒下。）

第五幕

●第一場 ——————————————— P. 109

P. 109

過了一會兒，普洛斯帕羅的洞穴前面。普洛斯帕羅上，穿著他的法袍，後面跟隨著愛麗兒。

普洛斯帕羅：我的計畫即將大功告成。我的法術奏效，我的精靈聽話，所有的事情都按部就班進行。現在幾點了？

愛麗兒：六點，你說我們的工作會在這個時候結束。

普洛斯帕羅：當我興起暴風雨的時候，我的確說過。告訴我，精靈，國王和他的跟隨者現在怎麼樣了？

愛麗兒：關在一起，和你離開的時候一樣。他們在洞穴附近的小樹林動彈不得，除非你放了他們。國王、他的弟弟、還有你的弟弟都焦慮不堪。其他的人為他們哭泣，淚中充滿了哀傷和沮喪。其中哭的最傷心的是那個你說的「善良老臣貢札羅」。他的淚從鬍子流下，像冬天的雨從茅草屋簷落下一般。你的法術太強大了，如果你現在看到他們，一定也會深受觸動。

普洛斯帕羅：你這麼認為嗎，精靈？

愛麗兒：如果我是人類的話，主人，我可能就會。

普洛斯帕羅：那我也會。如果連你這樣無形體的精靈都會憐憫他們，我當然也會。去放了他們吧，愛麗兒。我會解開我的咒語，讓他們恢復知覺，而他們將會再次恢復正常。

愛麗兒：我去把他們帶過來，主人。

（愛麗兒下。）

普洛斯帕羅：山丘、小溪、樹林的精靈們！步履輕盈、隨著潮起潮落追逐不停的精靈們！夜半時分在綠地結草成環，讓羊群不敢接近的精靈們！儘管你們在仙界中位階不高，但在你們的幫助之下，我遮蔽了中午的太陽、召喚了狂風前來、讓綠海藍天風雨交加。我得以將結實的橡樹以閃電劈成兩半，墓碑在我的命令下開棺，喚醒了裡面的長眠者。但是，現在我將要放棄這些強大的法術，僅僅只再需要一些天上的音樂，感動他們的知覺，我就會將我的法杖斷成兩節，並將之埋在適當的地方，也會將我的魔法書籍投入大海的最深處。（莊嚴的音樂響起。愛麗兒上，跟隨著宛若神智不清者一般舉止怪異的阿隆佐。貢札羅在後面照料他。瑟拜士梯安和安東尼奧也憂慮失常，後面跟著照顧他們的阿特利安和法朗西斯科，他們都出神地進入普洛斯帕羅的法力圈範圍，呆立不動。普洛斯帕羅開口和他們說話。）讓莊嚴的音樂安慰傷痛的心，治癒頭骨下無用的大腦！全部都站好，因為你們都在我的咒語控制之下。神聖正直的貢札羅，我因為同情你而流淚。咒語很快就會解除，就像清晨融化夜晚的黑暗，你的知覺很快就會清除籠罩在你理智的烏雲。啊，我親愛的貢札羅，我的救命恩人，我會用言語和行動來報答你。阿隆佐，你對我和我的女兒相當殘忍，你的弟弟也助紂為虐；你的良心現在折磨著你，瑟拜士梯安！（對安東尼奧：）你，我的兄弟，我的血與肉，竟然讓野心阻礙了我們兄弟之情。儘管你天性如此，我還是會饒恕你。（貢札羅、阿隆佐、瑟拜士梯安和安東尼奧都逐漸地擺脫了魔咒。）他們慢慢恢復了知覺，現在他們都看不到我，即使看到也認不出來。愛麗兒，去把我的帽子和劍拿來，我要脫去我的法袍，以米蘭公爵的樣子出現在他們面前。快去，精靈，你快要自由了！

（愛麗兒一邊唱歌，一邊幫普洛斯帕羅著衣。）

愛麗兒：

蜜蜂吸吮的地方，我在那裡，

櫻草花瓣下，我躺著休息，

當貓頭鷹啼叫，我安睡於地，

我翩翩飛翔，乘著蝙蝠的羽翼，

快樂的，追隨夏天的逝去。

我現在當要快樂的、快樂的，

在樹枝下的花朵裡棲息。

普洛斯帕羅：我纖巧的愛麗兒！我會想念你的，但你值得你的自由。（他整理自己的衣容。）好，好，好。（再次對愛麗兒：）去國王的船上，要隱身。找到在甲板下睡覺的水手。當船長和水手頭目轉醒，把他們帶過來，請你快點去！

愛麗兒：在你的脈搏跳動兩下之前，我將劃過天空，去而復返。

（愛麗兒下。）

貢札羅：這個地方真折磨人，充滿了麻煩、怪異、奇特，願上天的力量引導我們離開這個可怕的國度！

普洛斯帕羅（面對阿隆佐）：看清楚，國王，為人陷害的米蘭公爵——普洛斯帕羅在此！為了向您證明我是血肉之軀，而非幽魂對您說話，讓我擁抱您的身軀。（他擁抱阿隆佐。）歡迎您。

阿隆佐：我不知道你是不是真的普洛斯帕羅，你的脈搏像人類一樣跳動，看見你之後，我無名的瘋狂就消失了。如果這一切都是真實的話，這真是一個非常奇特的故事。我不再要求米蘭對我朝貢，我只求你饒恕我的罪過。但是，普洛斯帕羅是怎麼活下來的，又是如何出現在這裡呢？

普洛斯帕羅（轉向貢札羅）：首先，高貴的朋友，先讓我擁抱年邁的你，你的尊貴無人可比擬。

貢札羅（困惑）：我不知道這一切是真是假。

普洛斯帕羅：你還深陷這座島嶼的魔咒，讓你無從分辨真假。歡迎，我的朋友們。（對瑟拜士梯安和安東尼奧竊語：）然而你們這一對惡人，如果我願意的話，我會在國王面前揭穿你們叛國的惡行，但是暫時，我還不會這麼做。

瑟拜士梯安（竊語）：這是惡靈在說話！

普洛斯帕羅：不！（對安東尼奧：）至於你，你這個邪惡的人，稱呼你「兄弟」會弄髒了我的嘴。但是我原諒你，我要求你歸還我的王國，你完全沒有選擇的餘地。

阿隆佐：如果你真的是普洛斯帕羅，告訴我們你是如何得救的，又是如何在這裡遇到我們的。三小時前，我們遇到了船難，讓我失去了我親愛的兒子菲迪南。

普洛斯帕羅：國王，我很抱歉，我認為您並沒有尋求耐心的幫助。

阿隆佐：失去的已經無法挽回，耐心也於事無補。

普洛斯帕羅：我和您一樣也曾經失去過，我尋求忍耐的幫助，現在我安守天命。

阿隆佐：你也有同樣的遭遇？

普洛斯帕羅：和您一樣的重大打擊，我已經失去了我的女兒。
（當然，他意味的是女兒已經要嫁人。）

阿隆佐：女兒？啊，上天啊！噢，如果他們都像國王和王后一樣住在那不勒斯的話那有多好！你是何時失去女兒的？

普洛斯帕羅：在最近這場暴風雨。（他改變話題。）我看見這些大臣們到現在都相當驚訝，他們很難相信眼前所見的一切，但清楚知道我就是普洛斯帕羅，我就是當年被逐出米蘭的公爵，我就在你們發生船難的地方登上的陸岸。目前知道這樣就足夠了，因為說來話長。各位，歡迎你們，這個洞穴就是我的宮殿，我只有幾位侍從，沒有臣民。請看看裡面，既然你們回到了我的王國，我會用一樣好的東西來招待你們，讓你們賓至如歸，就像我的王國帶給我的安慰。

（普洛斯帕羅讓他們看見了菲迪南和米蘭達，兩人正在洞穴內下棋。）

阿隆佐：如果這是這座島引起的幻影的話，我將失去我親愛的兒子兩次！

瑟拜士梯安：這是天上的奇蹟！

菲迪南（驚訝地看到阿隆佐還活著）：大海雖然恐怖，但卻仁慈，我錯怪大海了。

阿隆佐：但願一個快樂父親的祝福可以永遠保佑你，你是怎麼來到這裡的？

米蘭達：啊，真是奇蹟！這麼多美善的人出現在我眼前！人類真是美麗！啊，這個美麗的新世界，有這樣的人兒住在這裡！

普洛斯帕羅：對你來說是一個嶄新的世界。

阿隆佐（對菲迪南）：和你一起對弈的女子是何人？你認識她絕不會超過三個小時。她是不是將我們分開後又讓我們相聚的女神？

菲迪南：陛下，她是人間女子。因為上帝的恩惠，她現在是我的妻子，我選擇她的時候沒有問過父親的意見，因為我當時不知道我還有父親。她是鼎鼎有名的米蘭公爵之女，我時常聽聞他的名號，卻從未見過他一面；我從米蘭公爵那裡獲得了我的第二生命，這位淑女讓他成為我的第二個父親。

阿隆佐：我現在也是她的第二個父親了，但是我得向我的孩子請求原諒，對我來說很不尋常！

普洛斯帕羅：好了，陛下，過去令人傷心的回憶就別再提了。

貢札羅：我內心在流淚，否則我早就開口說話了。天上的諸神啊，請俯視人間，請為這對新人戴上祝福的皇冠吧。

阿隆佐：阿門！貢札羅。

貢札羅：米蘭公爵被逐出國度，現在他的子孫將成為那不勒斯的國王嗎？啊，真令人高興，這得用金字在石板上銘記下來：

在一場航程中，克拉莉貝兒在突尼斯找到了她的丈夫，

而她的兄弟菲迪南在迷路的過程中找到了他的妻子。

普洛斯帕羅在一座貧瘠的島上找回了他的王國，

而我們都找回了我們自己。

阿隆佐：讓我握著你的手，那些不願看到我們快樂的人，讓哀痛與悲傷充滿他們的心靈！

貢札羅：如您所願，阿門！*（愛麗兒上，後面跟著表情驚訝的船長和水手頭目。）*啊，看啊，陛下，我們的人更多了！我就說如果這島上有絞刑台的話，這些傢伙就一定不會淹死。你們現在這樣安靜，不是嗎？在船上可是咒罵了半天！有什麼消息呢？

水手頭目：最好的消息就是我們平安地找到了我們的國王和他的臣子。接下來就是找到了我們的船，她三小時前還是四分五裂的，現在卻完好如初！

愛麗兒（對普洛斯帕羅竊語）：主人，這些都是我離開之後所做的。

普洛斯帕羅（對愛麗兒竊語）：我聰明的精靈！

阿隆佐：事情是愈來愈奇怪了。你說，你是怎麼找到這裡的？

水手頭目：陛下，如果我是醒著的，我想我會告訴你究竟發生什麼事。我們睡得很熟，後來，我也不知道怎麼回事，我們都卡在甲板下了。然後就在不久之前，很多奇怪的聲音傳來，狂吼、尖叫、咆哮、絞鍊聲還有很多奇怪的聲音。這些可怕的聲音嚇醒了我們，忽然間，我們都自由了！然後我們就看到了我們華麗無畏的皇家船隻，我們船長看到她之後，高興得跳起來了。後來，好像作夢一樣，我們離開了其他人員，不知不覺地被帶到這裡來。

愛麗兒（對普洛斯帕羅）：做的不錯吧？

普洛斯帕羅（對愛麗兒）：做得太好了！你就要自由了。

阿隆佐：得要有神諭才能解釋這一切。

普洛斯帕羅：陛下，別再自尋煩惱了。不久的將來，當我們有空的時候，我會——向您解釋清楚。在那之前，讓我們想想快樂的事，快樂起來吧。來吧，忠誠的精靈，放了卡列班和他的同黨吧，解開咒語的時候到了。(*愛麗兒下。普洛斯帕羅轉向阿隆佐。*)您覺得如何呢，我高尚的陛下？還有一些人沒有回來。

(*愛麗兒回來，帶著卡列班、斯蒂芬諾和屈林鳩羅，他們仍穿著偷來的衣服。*)

斯蒂芬諾(*仍帶有醉意，神智不清*)：每個人都要幫助別人，不要只照顧自己。一切都是運氣！怪物，要勇敢！

屈林鳩羅：如果我看到的是真的，這景象真可觀！

卡列班(*崇拜每個人*)：啊，惡魔！這些真是美麗的精靈！我的主人真是好看，我怕他會懲罰我。

瑟拜士梯安：哈，哈！這些是什麼東西啊，安東尼奧？可以用錢買嗎？

安東尼奧：或許吧。(*看著卡列班*)這個傢伙很奇特，應該可以很容易賣吧。

普洛斯帕羅：看看這些人所穿的衣服，各位。再評斷他們是否是誠實的人。(*手指卡列班*)這個醜陋的惡棍，他的母親是個女巫，強大到可以操縱月亮和潮汐。這三個人偷走了我的東西，而這怪物還策畫想要謀殺我。這兩個是你的人，但這黑暗的傢伙(*指著卡列班*)屬於我。

卡列班：我會被捏到死為止！

阿隆佐：這不是斯蒂芬諾，我那酗酒的廚師嗎？

瑟拜士梯安：很顯然地，他還在酒醉中，他是從哪裡找到酒喝的？

阿隆佐：屈林鳩羅也醉醺醺的，這個烈酒是哪來的？（對屈林鳩羅：）你怎麼醉成這樣？

屈林鳩羅：自從離開您後，我就醉成這樣了，我醉到連蒼蠅都不敢接近我！

普洛斯帕羅（對卡列班）：帶著你的同伴到我洞穴來，如果你要我原諒你，最好乖乖的。

卡列班：主人，我會的。從現在開始我會聰明點並且好好服侍你，我真是個笨蛋，竟然把酒鬼當作神，崇拜這樣的蠢貨！

普洛斯帕羅：快點去吧。

阿隆佐：把拿來的東西還回原處。

瑟拜士梯安：是偷來的東西。

普洛斯帕羅（對阿隆佐）：陛下，我邀請您和您的追隨者進入寒舍，您可以好好休息。晚上，我再好好與您談談，讓時光快點流逝。我會告訴您我的故事，還有我在這座島上遭遇的一切細節。明天早上我會送您上船，回到那不勒斯去，希望我們的子女可以在那裡舉行婚禮。之後我會回到米蘭，度過餘生。

阿隆佐：我期待聽你的故事，一定相當奇特。

普洛斯帕羅：我會將全部都告訴您，並保證您的回程風平浪靜，讓您迅速地趕上已經遠離的皇室船艦。（對愛麗兒竊語：）這些要交給你處理，我的愛麗兒。然後你就可以像風一樣自由了，珍重再見！（對所有人，指著他的洞穴：）如果各位願意的話，現在請跟我來。

（全體下。）

後記

●普洛斯帕羅致詞 ──────── P. 125

現在我的法術都已揚棄，
唯一的力量僅有我自己，
我是個弱者，一點不假，
我必須被你禁錮在這裡，
或是你們允許我回到故里。
既然我已重拾公爵的權力，
並且寬恕我的兄弟，
請別讓我待在這貧瘠之島，
請讓我從我的枷鎖中解脫。
藉由你們的雙手解除這魔咒，
你們有罪過也希望被寬恕，
就讓你們的掌聲助我獲得自由。

（普洛斯帕羅下。）

第五幕

第一場

Literary Glossary • 文學詞彙表

aside 竊語

一種台詞。演員在台上講此台詞時，其他角色是聽不見的。角色通常藉由竊語來向觀眾抒發內心感受。

■ Although she appeared to be calm, the heroine's **aside** revealed her inner terror.
雖然女主角看似冷靜，但她的**竊語**透露出她內在的恐懼。

backstage 後台

一個戲院空間。演員都在此處準備上台，舞台布景也存放此處。

■ Before entering, the villain impatiently waited **backstage**.
在上台前，壞人在**後台**焦躁地等待。

cast 演員；卡司陣容

戲劇的全體演出人員。

■ The entire **cast** must attend tonight's dress rehearsal.
全體演員必須參加今晚的正式排練。

character 角色

故事或戲劇中虛構的人物。

■ Mighty Mouse is one of my favorite cartoon **characters**.
太空飛鼠是我最愛的卡通**人物**之一。

climax 劇情高峰

戲劇或小說中主要衝突的結局。

■ The outlaw's capture made an exciting **climax** to the story.
逃犯落網成為故事中最刺激的**精彩情節**。

comedy 喜劇

有趣好笑的戲劇、電影和電視劇，並有快樂完美的結局。

- My friends and I always enjoy a Jim Carrey **comedy**.
  我朋友和我總是很喜歡金凱瑞演的**喜劇**。

conflict 戲劇衝突

故事主要的角色較量、勢力對抗或想法衝突。

- *Dr. Jekyll and Mr. Hyde* illustrates the **conflict** between good and evil.
  《變身怪醫》描述善惡之間的**衝突**。

conclusion 尾聲

解決情節衝突的方法，使故事結束。

- That play's **conclusion** was very satisfying. Every conflict was
  resolved. 該劇的**結局**十分令人滿意，所有的衝突都被圓滿解決。

dialogue 對白

小說或戲劇角色所說的話語。

- Amusing **dialogue** is an important element of most comedies.
  有趣的**對白**是大多喜劇中一項重要的元素。

drama 戲劇

故事，通常非喜劇類型，特別是寫來讓演員在戲劇或電影中演出。

- The TV **drama** about spies was very suspenseful.
  那齣關於間諜的電視**劇**非常懸疑。

event 事件

發生的事情；特別的事。

- The most exciting **event** in the story was the surprise ending.
  故事中最精彩的**事件**是意外的結局。

introduction 簡介

一篇簡短的文章，呈現並解釋小說或戲劇的劇情。

■ The **introduction** to *Frankenstein* is in the form of a letter.
《科學怪人》的**簡介**是以信件的型式呈現。

motive 動機

一股內在或外在的力量，迫使角色做出某些事情。

■ What was that character's **motive** for telling a lie?
那個角色說謊的**動機**為何？

passage 段落

書寫作品的部分內容，範圍短至一行，長至幾段。

■ His favorite **passage** from the book described the author's childhood.
他在書中最喜歡的**段落**描述了該作者的童年。

playwright 劇作家

戲劇的作者。

■ William Shakespeare is the world's most famous **playwright**.
威廉莎士比亞是世界上最知名的**劇作家**。

plot 情節

故事或戲劇中一連串的因果事件，導致最終結局。

■ The **plot** of that mystery story is filled with action.
該推理故事的**情節**充滿打鬥。

point of view 觀點

由角色的心理層面來看待故事發展的狀況。

■ The father's **point of view** about elopement was quite different from the daughter's. 父親對於私奔的**看法**與女兒迥然不同。

prologue 序幕

在戲劇第一幕開始前的介紹。

- The playwright described the main characters in the **prologue** to the play.

  劇作家在**序幕**中描述了主要角色。

quotation 名句

被引述的文句；某角色所說的詞語；在引號內的文字。

- A popular **quotation** from *Julius Caesar* begins, "Friends, Romans, countrymen . . ."

  《凱薩大帝》中**常被引用的文句**開頭是：「各位朋友，各位羅馬人，各位同胞⋯⋯」。

role 角色

演員在劇中揣摩表演的人物。

- Who would you like to see play the **role** of Romeo?

  你想看誰飾演羅密歐這個**角色**呢？

sequence 順序

故事或事件發生的時序。

- Sometimes actors rehearse their scenes out of **sequence**.

  演員有時會**不按順序**排練他們出場的戲。

setting 情節背景

故事發生的地點與時間。

- This play's **setting** is New York in the 1940s.

  戲劇的**背景設定**於 1940 年代的紐約。

soliloquy 獨白

角色向觀眾發表想法的一番言論，猶如自言自語。

- One famous **soliloquy** is Hamlet's speech that begins, "To be, or not to be . . ."
  哈姆雷特最知名的**獨白**是：「生，抑或是死……」。

---

symbol 象徵

用以代表其他事物的人或物。

- In Hawthorne's famous novel, the scarlet letter is a **symbol** for adultery.
  在霍桑知名的小說中，紅字是姦淫罪的**象徵**。

---

theme 主題

戲劇或小說的主要意義；中心思想。

- Ambition and revenge are common **themes** in Shakespeare's plays.
  在莎士比亞的劇作中，雄心壯志與報復是常見的**主題**。

---

tragedy 悲劇

嚴肅且有悲傷結局的戲劇。

- *Macbeth*, the shortest of Shakespeare's plays, is a **tragedy**.
  莎士比亞最短的劇作《馬克白》是部**悲劇**。